A TORN PAIGE

L. ROSE

PROLOGUE

I floated in the darkened sky looking below to the dirt mound surrounded by woods. I watched and waited for something to happen, as if I expected a situation. And when I saw the dirt shift, little rocks and soil tumbling to the side, I knew what I was waiting for.

I knew it as well as the next breath I needed.

Dirty hands popped through the earth. They clawed out of the ground, digging their way free.

Fear clenched my stomach, despite knowing I shouldn't be scared.

The scene was surreal.

A head broke free next and tipped back. A growl shuddered through the area. Wild red eyes took in everything. It was a woman. Her light-colored hair was either blonde or white, but filthy from the muck. She pushed at the dirt and then leaped from the hole she'd been buried in. As she landed in a crouch, her eyes frantically darted this way and that. Her head tipped again, her nostrils flaring. She scented her surroundings.

Another growl rumbled from her, tore from her. The sound almost animalistic.

The dress covering her small frame was in tatters.

My stomach tightened when I saw her clutch at her own

gut as she slowly stood, as if I could feel the hunger eating away at her.

The wind brushed through the area, her hair and dress swaying in the breeze. Suddenly, she spun right and crouched again. A low, humming rumble echoed out of her mud-caked mouth and into the woods.

Again, fear bombarded me.

The woman looked crazed. Her body tensed when we heard a branch break close by. Her upper lip pulled back in a snarl, a warning, and I felt mine doing the same.

Into the small clearing stepped a....

Confusion swamped me. I should know what it was, but I couldn't place it in my mind. The animal looked like a dog, but it was different. Bigger. Four times bigger than any dog I'd seen. Its body was built like a tank, even under the thick fur I could see each muscle pull while it slowly took step after step toward the woman. Its bright red eyes glowed back at her.

The animal let loose its own growl, but the full force of it was obstructed by something it carried in its mouth.

The woman stayed perfectly still, but I could tell she was ready to pounce if she needed to. If a fight was to be had, she was ready. She hadn't survived being buried for nothing. There was a reason everything happened.

There had to be.

The animal went down on its legs as it drew closer and then belly crawled the rest of the way to her. The woman's head tilted to the side as if confused, and again she scented the air with a big breath in. Another growl erupted from within her when hunger stabbed her stomach once more.

How I knew it, I wasn't sure.

But I knew it with the clarity of my own hunger.

The animal dropped what was in its mouth, nosed it toward her, and then retreated a little. Sitting, it watched her, looking from the woman to what lay in front of her.

My focus landed on the item it dropped, and my eyes widened.

It was an arm.

An arm from a human body.

The woman dove at it, picking it up before the animal could withdraw the offering. She scooted back, and while keeping her eyes on the animal, she lifted the arm, sniffed it and....

Oh, God.

She opened her mouth wide before biting into the flesh. Blood ran down around her lips. The kill must have been fresh. She moaned as she swallowed the first bite. It had sated the hunger, but only a little, so she took off another chunk using her teeth, not caring it coated her mouth and clothes in more blood, or that she was eating human flesh in the first place.

The animal stood and edged closer to the woman. She watched it with wary eyes and growled once when it sat beside her.

I should have been disgusted.

Even scared.

But I wasn't.

I wasn't because I knew.

I knew the woman had been reborn into something else, and the animal at her side was there to help her.

I knew it all... because I was her.

CHAPTER ONE
PAIGE

I jolted awake, flying to sit upright on my bed. The sheets tumbled to my waist as I attempted to control the erratic rise and fall of my chest. Not exactly breathing, because I didn't need to.

That damn dream.

My sleeping pattern had also been altered. I didn't need much, only a few hours every couple of days, but when I did, that same dream played with my mind.

Six months had gone by since that night.

The night I found myself waking and starving for human flesh.

I didn't know how it happened, if I was attacked, kidnapped, or killed. It took me a few days to come back to my old self—my memories and life before that night finally clearing in my mind. Everything except what led to me being buried. It was as if that part of my memory was erased.

I hated not knowing who had done it or why.

I didn't even know exactly what I had become... but if I was to guess, it would be a ghoul. I'd read enough urban fantasy to take a stab in the dark at it, and besides, Google somewhat helped me narrow it down. I didn't want to suck someone's blood dry, I didn't turn hairy every full moon, I didn't have wings, and I didn't have a hunger for brains alone. I liked to consume human meat. If I didn't have it at least once a week, my moods changed when the gut-wrenching hunger started deep inside me. On top of the whole "human flesh" thing, was that my non-beating heart was pretty much a dead giveaway with the ghoul theory.

Hell, before I was reborn into whatever I was, I didn't even know there were *others* in the world. I'd always thought vampires, werewolves, witches, fae, and demons were the things of fairy tales and romance stories. Then again, I hadn't actually met any other species, but I took a big guess that there were more than just humans in the world or else, how was I created? I guess Mom had always been wrong when she used to say, "Paige, why do you read that nonsense? It'll never teach you anything."

The bonus side of being undead—an assumption made with the lack of a beating organ—was that I didn't get my period. In fact, I didn't need to visit the bathroom at all besides to shower. I worked out, I still sweated, which was weird, and I also… became wet when I was turned on. Found that out one night when I was out clubbing and was attracted to someone who took me home for the night. I blessed anyone who would listen for *that* part of me to still be working. If it hadn't, it would have been one uncomfortable experience for both of us. Not that I saw him ever again.

Needless to say, everything was different. I wasn't sure how my brain still functioned when just about the rest of my body wasn't. Though, I was grateful for having my memories.

Especially when I remembered who I was and who my family was.

Now, between working as a barista in a local coffee shop, I spent the rest of my time hunting for the person who'd changed me. I wanted to know with what purpose they'd done it.

There had to be a reason behind the act of ending my life, so I was reborn into what I was.

Sighing, a normal habit of mine, I slipped the sheet off the rest of my body and stretched. Ezra must have heard my movement as he came bounding into my room. I gave him a sleepy smile and bent to rub my hands over his body.

I would have been lost even more without the help of Ezra —the animal who had been at my side when I woke. I still didn't know exactly what he was, but I knew he was special and happy to stick by my side, helping me feed in those first few nights when I wasn't myself.

Since then, Ezra taught me how to hunt my own food.

Hunt.

I hunted humans to eat. *Warm human flesh, fresh from a kill is what I like best. However, if it's a couple of days old, I'm still good with it, but anything over that I can't stomach.* Usually a thought like that would have churned my gut, or I would have just thrown up. But the squeamishness was all behind me now.

It had to be done. I had to eat human flesh or I would slowly starve. I wouldn't say to death, because I wasn't sure what could kill me. But it was to a point where I worried I'd turn crazed and kill someone. Even loved ones, and I wouldn't risk that. So I made sure I hunted those who deserved it. Those who killed and raped.

Ezra helped me find them and take them down. I didn't know how he did it, but I was grateful to have him at my side.

Even though we couldn't talk to one another, we were still in sync. He knew how I was feeling, what I needed, and somehow understood what I said. I just couldn't speak animal. If he *was* an animal. I mean, he was. I just wasn't sure if he was any type that lived on Earth.

Still, I loved him no matter.

My life had changed, but I was still the same person on the inside—in my dead heart and soul. At first, because I didn't know what I was, I'd contemplated ending my life. What kept me going and not giving in to those dark thoughts were my family and Ezra.

Smiling down at him, I said, "Come on. I better get ready before we're late to meet Yasmin." He actually rolled his eyes at me. He didn't mind going to my sister's place because he loved playing with her kids. But that night my sister had wanted to go out for dinner to celebrate her husband's promotion, so Ezra was annoyed he wouldn't be getting the attention from them. Because even though Ezra could transform himself from his massive natural form—which I was yet to figure out exactly what he was in his real form since there were so many creatures he could resemble or ones I'd read up on without a picture for reference online—into a newfoundland breed of a dog, which, thanks to Google, I was able to recognize. The place we were going to didn't allow animals. That meant he would have to go unseen to the human eye.

Both of those talents I discovered within a few weeks of my return.

I'd been used to seeing him in his monstrous form, where his fur was wild and scruffy, his height reaching the top of my shoulders. He had glowing eyes and razor-sharp teeth. His mouth also revealed two long, sharp fangs jutting out and over his bottom lip, and then there were the spikes that ran down his spine. The night he first transformed his body into a canine form was when I'd told him I was going out, without him, to see my sister after finally feeling normal for the first time. He'd stood in front of the door and refused to move. I'd told him he couldn't go because everyone would have a fit at me for bringing him looking like he was—a scary beast. He'd huffed at me, and I'd tumbled back when his body altered, changed, and mutated to the newfoundland size.

The first time I'd discovered he could become invisible to humans was when we were out hunting. I was down at one end of the alley and Ezra at the other. I'd scented the fresh blood on my prey's hands, even though they seemed clean.

"Who did you kill?" I'd asked.

The man had sneered. "What are you talking about?"

"Wife?" I'd questioned and didn't get a reaction. "Sister?" I'd pressed and got nothing. "Employer?" Zilch. "Girlfriend?" He'd winced. I'd clicked my tongue, shaking my head. "Why?"

His face had contorted with rage. "She wouldn't give me money. Kept it all to herself, the greedy bitch."

"Seriously? You killed her over money?"

He'd kept backing up toward Ezra, as if he couldn't see the threat behind him each time he looked over his shoulder to see if he had a clear run.

I'd paused, tilted my head, and glanced behind him to Ezra. "He can't see you, can he?"

The guy had spun around, looking everywhere. I'd started laughing.

"What are you laughing at?" the man had screeched. His eyes wide in fear, finally.

I'd grinned. "Wow, I wish I could see your face if you saw what was behind you."

Fascinated, I'd watched as Ezra's body shimmered. He'd let out a snorted snuffle, and the man spun his way. He'd screamed, the scent of urine hitting my nose, and then he'd tried to run my way.

Of course, he hadn't expected my strength. He'd thought

the gun in my grip was all I'd had to protect myself... well, besides Ezra. So he hadn't expected me to lower the gun, tuck it into the waist of my jeans, and then brace myself as he got closer. His chest had heaved with every breath he took; panic had him begging even before he'd reached me.

It was too late. He could beg all he wanted, but he'd taken a life, so his wasn't worth living either.

Ezra's nose burrowed under my hand, bringing me from my thoughts. "Eww, cooties," I complained with a laugh. He then, of course, got close and snorted into my hand on purpose. Just to be grosser, he licked all of my hand as I tried, while laughing still, to push him back. Wrapping my arms around his neck, I slid off my bed and tackled him to the ground. "You're a monster." His lips pulled back off his razor-sharp teeth, as if smiling. I groaned, laughing the word, "Whatever." I bounced up to my feet. "I'll get a quick shower in. Then we'd better move it."

After showering, I got ready. Since it was a fancy restaurant, where I would eat a little food since I still needed some type of sustenance between my "other" meals to help sedate my new side, I chose a black dress and heels to match my long dark hair and eyes. I'd even applied a little makeup to cover the paleness of my skin. I'd brought a long red jacket to go over the top since it was cold out. Not that the change in weather bothered me, but it made me look normal since others would have warmer clothing on.

The drive didn't take long. As I turned the corner to the restaurant, I slammed on the brakes. Ezra, in his canine form, went flying forward, only managing to brace at the end, so he didn't crash through the windshield. Thankfully no one was behind me. Then again, the streets were quiet in this area, something that I should have noticed already.

My heart would have taken off in flight if it could.

Instead, dread caused my hands to shake slightly. I quickly pulled my car off to the side of the road and parked. With Ezra at my heels, I climbed out. My hand went to the top of his head as he moved to my side. The street was usually a busy spot, bustling with people walking, driving, or heading into the numerous shops around. Instead, the place was quiet. No one was around except for three men dressed in black and armed to hell, who stood out the front of where my family was. They were barricaded by cars. Something had happened inside that restaurant, and I needed to find out what.

Something was wrong.

Very wrong.

I shivered in fear, a reaction I hadn't experienced in a long time.

Still, no matter what was happening, I was going in there to help my sister. My upper lip pulled back from my teeth in a silent snarl. No one hurt my sister.

With a purpose-filled stride, I made my way over, and as I stepped up to the back of the group of men, something caused my body to hum. Ignoring it, I kept going, stopping beside one of the men at the front.

Startled, the guy behind them tried to grab my arm with a surprised "Hey." But I dodged it.

The man I stood beside stopped talking to the guy next to him, noticing his other man calling out. He glanced over his shoulder to his man before doing a double take, his gaze landing on me. Actually, all of them were looking down at me, since they were damn tall, with wide eyes. The man at my side slowly slid his gaze all the way down my body and then back up. He looked about midthirties. His light blue eyes narrowed, and he jerkily ran a hand over his long black hair. With a quick glance, I took him in. His shoulders were wide, and I could see the definition his body held under his black Henley long-sleeve top. His jeans also sat snugly against his butt—one I wouldn't mind grabbing. *So wrong, Paige.*

"What's going on in there?" I asked, getting back on track to the situation.

He opened his mouth, snapped it closed, and then glowered. "Who are you?" Not waiting for an answer, he spun and demanded, "Smith, how did she get through your ward?"

Ward? That was a spell, right? Which meant I wasn't dealing with normal humans. An excited thrill ran up my spine. I hadn't yet met any *others*. Maybe I should have guessed they were different from the power that tingled over my skin. But I'd been distracted by the worry I held for my sister.

"I don't know, sir," Smith answered. I glanced at him, at his strange gray gaze and dark blond hair, which was buzzed at the sides and back, but longer and messy on top. He was built smaller in size than the other two, but still impressive, and I had a feeling his stamina would be good.... Why I even thought that I didn't know because it wasn't the time. It also wasn't time to get lost in his warm, soft eyes. He seemed like the nicer out of all of them. Smith, he'd been called. I had to remember it.

Ezra huffed from my side, and I caught Mr. In Charge's eyes lasered down on him.

No matter who or what they were, they were keeping me from helping my family. Since I was sick of waiting, I asked again, "*What's* going on in there?"

He pulled his piercing gaze back up to me. "You need to leave, little girl. Take your dog and go."

Little girl? I knew I looked young but being called a little girl was just an insult.

Annoyance dipped my brows. I hummed and tapped my chin, then shook my head. Behind us, Smith chuckled. "I don't think so. Now, are you going to answer *my* question?"

"No," he clipped, crossing his arms over his broad chest. "Smith?" he called.

"I would have guessed human, but she doesn't have a heartbeat. Then I'd have thought one of yours, but that's wrong. She feels different."

"You're right," he bit out, and I had a feeling he didn't like puzzles or that I'd just walked into his world. I swung my gaze around at them. They could tell I didn't have a heartbeat. Interesting. Now I was certain they were different like me.

"I can't pick it up either. Just make her leave," a guy growled out roughly.

Ezra snarled just as low.

I faced the man who'd spoken, the one on the other side of whoever "sir" was. His green, narrowed stare held mine when I told him, "I wouldn't try to make me leave, because I won't. My sister is in there with her family, and *I* want to know what's going on." The guy's upper lip raised. He was bigger than all of them, yet it looked good on him. Too good with his shaggy dark-brown hair. I tore my gaze away after I quickly coughed into my hand, "Dick." His eyes flashed wide for a second, but I saw it. I deemed his new name Mr. Arrogant.

Mr. In Charge said, "This isn't the time for hysterical family members—"

"Do I look hysterical?" Mimicking his stance, I crossed my arms over my chest. His gaze flicked down and then back up. Shit. I wished I'd worn my proper ass-kicking gear because I didn't think my black dress and heels were intimidating at all to these men. As well as my height and size. Sighing, I tried again, "Just please tell me what's going on in there, so I know what I'm walking into."

Mr. Arrogant man snorted. "You and your little doggie aren't going anywhere near there."

Ezra rumbled out another growl. I smiled. They would soon get a shock when they found out Ezra wasn't just a little doggie. The thought made me want to laugh. I didn't, of course. "Sure, okay. Guess I'm not going to get any answers anyway." I shrugged, turning. Smith moved aside for me with a pitying smile. I took one step by him and then spun back around, racing toward the entrance. The men shouted, cursed, and I even sensed one or two of them starting to come after me, until I called over my shoulder, "Ezra, keep them back."

Just before I walked through the front door, I glanced back to see Ezra standing in the pathway, his body shaking with the change as he grew and grew to his full size.

Then I heard before the door closed, "Fuck me. She has a hellhound."

So that's what Ezra was.

CHAPTER TWO

Once the door closed fully, I straightened my dress and moved toward, then around the front closed-off section and into the restaurant. I stopped and took in what was before me.

A man, at least that was what I presumed it was since his body was misshaped, stood beside a table of three kids and a couple, a gun pointing down at them. His other hand, with a second gun, was already aimed my way. He must have heard me coming.

"You move, I'll shoot them all."

I quickly took in the rest of the room. A lot of the tables were filled with employees, couples, or families cringing and crying as they held one another. My family was off to the left of the man. Eric, my sister's husband, held Yasmin close. Their kids, my niece and nephew, were on their laps, silently crying.

I blinked. My hands shot up in front of me. "Whoa, hold on a second. I just walked in here to meet my date. What's going on?"

The man scoffed. "Your date? And those guys out front didn't try to stop you?" His unbelieving gaze narrowed even more.

"Ah, yeah, they tried. But I wasn't listening to douches like that when I had a date to get to."

Loud snarling sounded from out the front. The ground

shook a little. People screamed.

Dammit, they'd better not hurt Ezra, or I'd kill them myself. My thoughts drifted to Ezra being a hellhound. How did those men know? Though, I had a feeling they knew a lot of things, maybe even what I was for certain.

Shit. It wasn't the time to contemplate stuff. I had to bring forward my acting skills. "Holy hell," I cried, clutching my chest. "What could that be?" I glanced over my shoulder and then back to Mr. Dickhead.

"Probably them, but they won't come in here and risk the hostages." His head tilted, probably wondering why he'd just told me that. His face darkened. "If you're here on a date, where is he?"

I glanced around, pretending to search for someone. My sister looked like she wanted to scream at me for being in there and acting like an idiot. Terror shined in her eyes. Though I suspected she knew I was different, she definitely knew I was strong and fast. But she didn't know why. How could she since I didn't have the answers for her. Would I tell her if I ever found out? Probably. We'd usually tell each other everything; however, I felt the need to avoid the subject of how I dug my way out of a grave and the details of my new diet... for now at least. For most of our lives, we'd only had each other. After our parents had died on a safari, and since Yasmin had been twenty at the time it happened, she looked after my sixteen-year-old self. Though, she would always say we looked after each other.

"Hell, he's not here." I stamped my foot. "Do you think he stood me up?"

Mr. Dickhead eyed me skeptically. "Maybe. Too bad for you. Now you're involved." He gestured with his gun. "Sit down over there and shut the fuck up."

I made my way over to the chair he pointed to, where a man and woman already sat at the table. As soon as my butt was on the chair, I raised my hand like I was in school.

Mr. Dickhead sighed. "What?" he clipped.

"Can I ask what's all this about? I know I'm late to the game, but will this take long? I'd like to find the asshole who stood me up and give him a piece of my mind."

Dickhead's brows shot up. "Really?"

I rolled my eyes. "Yes. No one stands me up." I waved my hand around flippantly. "So, what's this about?"

His jaw clenched, and his eyes... they swirled, going from light brown to black and then back again. Something was on the inside peeking out. Did that mean his body wasn't his own, or was it a part of him? Was whatever in him the reason he was misshapen and the reason for his long arms? His bumpy face?

What was I facing?

Would it be something I could beat?

I had to. I couldn't let the worry seep in. I had to beat him —*it*—so my family was safe.

He shook his head back and forth over and over, then suddenly stopped. He focussed on me, his gaze fully black.

His teeth flashed at me. "Pretty, pretty pet." His head twitched to the side. A gun fired, people screamed and shrieked, and then the wailing came. I didn't move. I couldn't. I was frozen, waiting for the pain to come, thinking he'd fired the gun at me. He didn't. More screams rang around the room, those frantic with terror.

It was then I saw the man with his family slumped forward over the table. Blood poured from his head onto the white cloth.

He'd shot a father in front of his family.

A father.

The wife bellowed through her pain, gripping her children to her. The kids sobbed, hiding their faces against their mother's body.

"Shut up!" Dickhead yelled.

Everyone did. Even the noise from outside silenced.

Please, please let Ezra be okay.

Dickhead had been watching me the whole time. Another twitch of his head. His nose lifted without his face moving up. He drew in the scent around him. "Hmm." He licked his lips. "Soon. Soon. Soon. She's dying. You will change and be mine."

Confusion rolled through my mind, but I let it slide and asked the one question I needed to know. "Why?"

"Why?" he screeched. "Why? Why? Why? Why?" He laughed then. "Because I was called. He wanted help. I was called, and he had second thoughts of shooting his boss. His boss. His boss. No one backs out of a deal with me."

A demon.

I rolled my thoughts through the many Google searches. I concluded it had to be a demon because it was all I could think of.

Fuck.

I'd never dealt with one before. I didn't know if I could. Hell, I'd never dealt with any other supernatural before, so no matter what, I was out of my element. Still, I had to try. I had to do something.

He licked his lips again, running his tongue slowly over his bottom lip. "I can taste your change. *Taste it.* Soon." He laughed gleefully and trained both weapons on me. "We leave. You come with me, and no one else gets hurt."

What did he mean by the change?

I'd already changed.

I stood and heard a yelp. I chanced a brief glance to my sister. Eric had a hand over her mouth. Tears filled her eyes. I closed my own. Turmoil sliced at my dead heart from the alarm I saw in her.

Because I knew, *knew* she would know I would do anything to stop people from dying.

Nodding, I straightened, opened my eyes, and stepped forward. "Okay. All right. I'll go." I walked toward him, and as soon as I was in grabbing distance, he reached forward with the gun still in his hand and took hold of my wrist. Spinning me, he placed me in front of him. His arm wound around my waist, drawing me back into his chest. I shuddered in disgust when I felt his warm breath on my neck.

"Yes. Soon, and then I will rule your people."

My people?

What did that mean?

I couldn't analyze his crazy words now, though.

"Everyone stay seated," he called out as he started backing toward the kitchen. I caught sight of Yasmin struggling within Eric's arms. I shook my head at her, and she slumped, defeated. Tears ran down her cheeks.

If I just got him outside, I could stop him. I would do something to make sure I was safe for my family. I couldn't let Yasmin lose me like we had our parents.

We were moving faster. I tripped, and he yanked me up. His grip was now painful around me.

A gun cocked from behind. The demon froze. "Where do you think you're going?" a deep voice, one I recognized as the Mr. In Charge out front, said.

The demon laughed. "You shoot me, she dies."

"She leaves with you, she dies" was his reply.

"We leave, we keep everyone else safe," I added my own tidbit.

The ground shook. Heavy pounding footfalls approached. Screams echoed around the room when the front of the building's glass shattered and Ezra came bounding in, skidding to a stop after he crashed through the divider from the front to the eating area.

I sighed in relief to see he was in one piece with a few scrapes and scratches.

"Shut up," the demon—as I was now convinced more than ever that was what he was—roared.

Fear stank up the room as people quieted down.

"Smith?" Mr. In Charge called.

A frazzled-looking Smith, with his hair sticking up all over the place, shuffled around Ezra's form. "Sorry, boss, he got away."

"Jesus," Mr. In Charge muttered. I really wish I knew his name because he certainly wasn't in charge of me.

"Any of you move, I will kill all the little humans," the demon growled.

Ezra snarled, just as Mr. Arrogant came to stand beside him. "Seems we have a standoff." The idiot smirked. "You only have your strength in that weak body. Leave now and you'll live to fight another day."

"She comes with me," he stated.

"She stays, demon," Mr. In Charge replied.

Ding, ding, ding, I was so right.

"Can we at least take this outside?" I asked.

"No," Mr. In Charge snapped.

"He gets you outside near his ley line, you're toast," Smith mentioned.

"Let her go," Mr. Arrogant demanded in a rough tone. A

tone I kind of liked. At least my lady bits did, but it wasn't the time to be appreciating it.

"She comes—"

I groaned, loud and long. "How long are we going to do this? Just shoot him already."

Everyone blinked slowly at me.

But no one goddamn shot him.

The demon cackled. "They won't risk you."

Fine, if they wouldn't risk me, I had to.

"Yasmin, look away," I said, and then I reached up to place my hands at the back of the demon's neck.

"Don't!" Mr. Arrogant barked.

My body jolted from the demon's gun at my side. I dug my fingers into his neck as he dropped one gun and placed his fingers against my neck.

"You kill me, I take your life," he warned.

For a second, I froze. It was all of a second because anger flamed inside me. I would not let him take me. I wouldn't die a second time.

With all my strength, I twisted in his arms. He tried to hold me tightly, but I managed to spin in his hold, grip his head, and squeeze. My body shook as he loaded bullet after bullet into me.

I screamed into his face, just before I ripped his head clear off his body.

Silence.

Deafening silence. So much so, my ears started ringing. The body crumpled in a heap at my feet, and I stared down at the head in my hands.

More terrified yells grew around me.

"Smith," Mr. In Charge bellowed.

Then more silence.

Blinking, I looked up and around. The humans in the room were frozen in place. Some had already tried to make a run for it.

A hand touched my arm. I flinched and faced Mr. In Charge.

"What's your name?" he asked calmly.

"What's yours?" I countered.

His lips thinned in annoyance or humor. Either way, I didn't care. My family was safe. I was safe. "Asher Evans."

I nodded once. "Paige Alice," I replied. "I—" I gasped. Pain, agonizing pain sliced through my chest, as if there was a hot poker drilling into my heart slowly. I dropped the head to clutch the area. Crying out, I fell to my knees.

"Paige," Asher called. "What is it?" He got to his knees beside me but was knocked back when Ezra arrived to stand over me. "Move, beast. Let me help her."

Ezra growled from the back of his throat, a threat and warning. I rolled to my side, curling up, panting through the tearing, the ripping happening inside me. Clenching my jaw, I closed my eyes tightly.

"Move," someone else ordered.

Ezra let out a howl and scratched at the floor as he moved over my body more.

Fire.

Fire so hot burned from within.

My eyes sprung wide along with my mouth as I screamed. I yelled so loud and long it hurt my throat, but that was nothing compared to what I felt inside.

Male voices yelled, threatened, and roared around me. I couldn't focus on any.

A bright white light flashed and then nothing but blackness.

CHAPTER THREE
ASHER

The council for the supernatural community had been founded thousands of years ago. For five decades I had been working for them as one of their soldiers, or as they classed us, even in training, their elite enforcers.

Under orders, we went to war when needed. We eliminated any lawbreaking citizens or anyone who risked our existence to the human race. We protected those who couldn't protect themselves, and we hunted demons to send them back to where they came from. It was only moments ago when the council had received a call about a demon causing havoc, and they sent us for the job. Evicting a demon from Earth was a piece of cake. Especially with our mixed group, something that no other elite group had.

I was the one who had approached the council after being there for a decade to see if they would accept a mixed-species group. At first, they quickly declined my idea, thinking it ridiculous. Four years after my first attempt, I asked again, and they allowed *one* group, my group, to try it. A test to see how things worked out. However, when they offered up a shifter for my first member, I was wary. I'd heard this shifter didn't work well with others. No matter how many shifter groups he'd teamed up with, he ended up on his own because of his asshole ways.

When I had seen Nate Felan, the shifter to our group, brutally fighting another shifter for intimidating a weaker opponent at the compound, I didn't second-guess the council's suggestion. I asked him if he would be interested in a position on the team. Nate and I had been working together for the last four decades.

Others had come into our group and either asked for a transfer, not liking Nate, or had died in battle.

The last and most recent addition to our small group was Alex Smith, a mage. He'd been with us for the last five years. Before he joined, I'd studied his file. He'd been top of his class and fresh out of magic school into the elite enforcers. He was full of power and intelligence, yet in many other ways, he was still young for his thirty years. Young in experience, but he was learning fast.

All of us aged differently, some not at all. Like Nate and me. We would stay at the age we appeared, in our late thirties, forever. Alex would age another ten years, but then his aging would stop there for him as well. We lived until we decided to leave this world, or died in war. We were the same in a lot of ways, yet we all thought and strategized differently, and worked well together. We'd seen a lot through our years. We were strong, feared and, at least Nate and I, had earned the respect of the council members for the work we'd done.

Nothing on this earth could surprise us anymore.

Until now.

I was good at blanking my expression, but when the shorter, sexy woman had stepped up beside me outside, I was shocked to the core, and I knew it showed. Then her quick wit and cool exterior impressed me, so I didn't notice everything there was about her. Not until Smith picked up she had no heartbeat. With my mind, I reached out to hers and tried to gain access, but it was impenetrable. What I did know was that she wasn't one of my kind. A vampire.

Which made me question what she could be.

As far as we knew, all other species that didn't contain a beating heart no longer existed.

There were demons, of course, but she didn't act like the soul-stealing monsters.

What made me more impressed was when she'd played us before she started for the front door. It was then my body reacted at the thought of the demon inside the restaurant getting his hands on her. My body woke from its decades of rest by fear creeping in, causing my gut to drop and my throat to thicken. I knew she'd entered the situation for her sister's sake, to make sure she'd be safe. I understood her reasoning because I'd do anything for my family and the team I worked with.

Still, I didn't think she understood the situation exactly or how much danger she was about to step into. Nate and I started to follow her. When she ordered her dog to keep us back, I wanted to throw my head back and laugh at the audacity the tiny woman showed. That was until her dog stepped in front of us and—I still couldn't believe it— changed into a goddamn hellhound.

If she wasn't a demon, then who else controlled hellhounds?

Would she be a danger to my crew?

What and who in the hell was she?

Christ, not even Nate could scent what she was, and he had the best damn nose in the business.

Nate shifted into his wolf form as my ears picked up on

what was being said inside. Only what I heard, I couldn't believe. The woman's acting was questionable, and I wasn't sure the demon would go with it, but he seemed to want to.

The ground shook as Nate and the hellhound collided.

"Smith, detain the animal without harm while Nate distracts him," I ordered. It was a simple spell for Alex. Before I could see him work his magic, I made my way around the side of the building.

My heightened hearing picked up a gun being fired. People screamed and cried. All I could think about was that I hoped, whoever had been shot—since the scent of blood was in the air—wasn't the woman who'd just walked in.

Moving through the back door, I listened carefully. The demon's attention stayed on the walking and talking woman. He wanted her, but why? I was determined to have an answer to that question soon.

I slipped through the kitchen doors just as the demon backed closer my way.

Raising my gun higher, I aimed at the back of his head. I cocked it and smirked when the demon froze. "Where do you think you're going?"

The demon laughed. "You shoot me, she dies."

I rolled my eyes. I wasn't stupid, and this wasn't the first time we'd played with demons. "She leaves with you, she dies."

"We leave, we keep everyone else safe," the woman added. She was still trying to save everyone else but herself. Christ, it touched my cold, dead heart.

The ground shook. Heavily pounding footfalls approached. Screams echoed around the room when glass shattered up front. The damn hellhound, what she called Ezra, came bounding in. It skidded to a stop after he crashed through the divider from the front waiting area to where we all were.

"Shut up," the demon roared around the room.

People quieted straightaway out of fear.

"Smith?" I called.

He stood just to the side and behind Ezra, seeming exasperated. "Sorry, boss, he got away."

"Jesus," I muttered.

"Any of you move, I will kill all the little humans," the demon growled.

Ezra snarled back as Nate, in human form, came to stand beside him.

"Seems we have a standoff." Nate smirked. "You only have your strength in that weak body. Leave now and you'll live to fight another day."

"She comes with me," he stated.

"She stays, demon," I replied, growing bored, but I wouldn't risk killing him with her in his arms.

"Can we at least take this outside?" the woman asked, her tone full of irritation.

"No," I snapped, shocked she wasn't scared even a little.

"He gets you outside near his ley line, you're toast," Smith mentioned.

"Let her go," I demanded roughly.

"She comes—"

The little woman groaned in annoyance. Shit, I wanted to laugh at her, but refrained. She then said, "How long are we going to do this? Just shoot him already."

All I could do was blink at her audacity.

The demon laughed. "They won't risk you."

"Yasmin, look away," the woman called out. My eyes widened as she reached up to place her hands at the back of his neck.

"Don't!" Nate barked, worry appearing in his tone.

Goddamn, her beautiful body jolted from the demon's gun at her side being fired shot after shot into her.

For the first time in centuries, I was frozen in place, watching her push her fingers into the demon's neck. He dropped one gun and covered her neck with his free hand.

"You kill me, I take your life," he warned.

Her face contorted into anger. A silent snarl pulled her upper lip from her teeth.

With strength I didn't know she'd have, she twisted in his arms, gripped his head and squeezed. Her body spasmed as he unloaded more rounds into her. I made a dive forward to help, as did Nate and Smith.

She screamed into his face, causing us to all pause, and then, *fuck me*, she tore his head right off his body.

Silence.

Utter silence.

My body hummed with the adrenaline running through my veins, and I put it down to the panic I'd felt for the woman. Never had I reacted like this for a victim. Why her?

Her chest rose and fell, but I couldn't feel or scent her breath. Was she even breathing?

The body dropped to the floor at her feet. Only I didn't take my eyes off her.

The humans around us started to yell once again.

"Smith," I yelled over the noise.

Within seconds, there was more silence.

The woman blinked a few times before raising her head

and gazing around, noting everyone but my team and her were frozen.

Gently, I reached out and touched her arm. She flinched but faced me with a calm, blank expression.

"What's your name?" I asked softly.

"What's yours?" she countered.

It was a struggle not to laugh. The woman was strong, and I needed answers. "Asher Evans."

She nodded once. "Paige Alice. I—" Paige's eyes widened as she gasped. The head slipped from her hands, and she clutched at her chest before falling to her knees.

"Paige," I called in alarm. "What is it?" I got to my knees beside her, only to be knocked on my ass when the hellhound barreled over to stand above her. "Move, beast," I snarled. "Let me help her."

"Move," Nate ordered, trying to shove Ezra off her.

He didn't budge; instead, he let out a howl and pawed at the floor as he stood more directly over her body.

Fuck.

I dug my hand into Ezra's neck and growled my own warning. If the beast didn't move, I would do it for him. Piece by piece.

I sensed Smith at my back, ready for my order.

To my surprise, Ezra backed off a little, his attention shifting to Paige, and ours followed. Her eyes popped wide, along with her mouth, and then she let out an ear-piercing scream. It was so damn loud and long, all of us had to cover our ears.

She stopped.

"Smith, calm her. Ezra, fucking move," I barked.

Nate shoved at him over and over, throwing threat after threat at the beast. Finally, he stepped back, one paw then the other. Smith and I reached her side at the same time, but before we could touch her, a bright white light flashed before us. Our bodies were thrown into the air, and we landed with a deafening crash onto the floor.

"What the hell was that?" I asked, my head spinning. Shit, I hadn't felt like that since I was a human and drunk. Slowly, I sat up. "Smith?"

"Magic of some sort, but I don't know what."

"Nate?" I called.

A mumbled response sounded from under the hellhound. It wasn't the time to laugh, but I had yet another urge to. As I rushed back to Paige's side, Ezra climbed to his feet, and I caught Nate shake his head as he sat up.

I stopped, hovering over Paige. She looked the same. Whatever happened hadn't caused her bodily harm. I tugged at a hole in her top. Even the wounds she'd had from the gunshots had healed quicker than any of us could have.

"Is she okay?" Smith asked, kneeling on the other side of her. Nate, who refused to go by his last name, stood by her feet.

"Stop," Nate shouted. We did. "Do you hear it?"

At his question, my ears picked up the extra, and loudest, heartbeat in the room. One I hadn't heard with all the others before. One that stood out more than the rest. We all glanced back down to Paige, knowing it was hers.

"But…." I didn't know what else to say.

"She didn't have one outside," Nate said.

"She didn't have one up until now," Smith added. "What is she?"

The hellhound came forward. It headbutted Nate out of the way and got close, sniffing Paige. He whimpered, then licked her face. I tried to shove his head away, but the bastard wouldn't move.

We all locked solid when she groaned.

"She's coming to," Smith muttered the obvious.

We all looked at each other. "You sure she's not one of your kind?" Nate asked.

I nodded. "She's not a vampire. I don't sense her as kin."

"So then what species doesn't have a beating heart one moment and then, in the next, does?" Nate asked.

"I—" Tensing, I felt a new pull in the room, as if something was drawing power. Ezra backed off Paige, whimpering. "Anyone?" I called roughly.

"Don't know," Smith replied.

"You all feel it?" Nate asked. He waved his hands above Paige. "I think it's coming from here."

"Nate, stop—" A surge of power pulsated out, sending us flying back once again, away from Paige. My head hit the wall as I crashed into it, causing my eyes to slam closed.

Opening them, I snarled at the figure standing over Paige.

"You'll not have her," I growled, my vampire side causing my voice to deepen, and I knew my eyes had bled to green.

Nate roared, shifting once more even as he stood and moved closer. The man over Paige wore a bored expression and ignored us. He bent and slid his arms under her.

"Smith," I barked.

"It's not working on him," he called back, a tinge of panic in his voice.

The guy slowly straightened with her in his arms, and Paige let out a mew of protest. Nate was still midshift and hadn't reached them yet, so I charged them myself. I had to see what we were up against. Once I was close, I reached for his throat, only to skid to a stop.

Paige's eyes shot wide. Her pupils bled from dark blue to glowing red with a black ring around them. Her body arched in his hold so dramatically he had to drop her.

She landed in a crouch, her palms flat to the ground. With her upper lip raised over her teeth, she let out a low hiss.

Holy Christ. What was she?

CHAPTER FOUR
NATE

I forced the change back into my human body, my clothes torn and tattered, but still covering most of me. I couldn't believe what I was seeing. The annoying yet cute Paige, whose scent had appealed to a part of me and my wolf deep inside when I'd first seen her, was something else, and I didn't have a fucking clue what.

She looked wild.

Her head lifted more. Her nostrils flared. She was scenting the air like an animal.

"Too many humans," the naked guy beside her commented.

"What do you mean?" Asher asked harshly.

"She'll kill them all. She's not herself. Been changed." Worry seeped into his tone while his hands fisted at his sides.

"Fuck," I snapped. "Smith, it's your time to shine."

His lips thinned, but he nodded. His eyes shone purple, his hands moving around in the air. The barest of seconds later, all the humans stood and started for the front exit.

"Erase their minds," I added. Smith lifted his chin toward me as he led the people out.

Paige let out a low-sounding snarl, her gaze glued to the glass-eyed people shuffling out the door. Her head twitched to the side, toward the naked guy, then back again. Her whole body tensed; she was preparing to make a run.

Asher had already sensed it and dove. His arms circled her waist, and he rolled them both backward. She screamed as her nails raked over Asher's arms, causing him to curse. I rushed over to them. Asher curled his legs up and over hers to hold them down. I perched over both Asher and Paige to grab her wrists and drag them down to the floor.

Asher grunted when her elbow connected with his rib. The crunch of his bones shattering under her strength tore around the emptying room.

"Hold her," he snapped, pain lacing his voice. Though, I knew his body would quickly heal.

"I'm fucking trying," I yelled. Her teeth gnashed up at me, her eyes narrowing, and if I had to guess, she was picturing my death. "Where in the hell is her hellhound? He might be able to calm her."

"He's over there," the naked guy stated from Paige's side with a gesture of his chin. Then he bent down and—*holy motherfucking shit*—the guy shoved the dead man's arm into Paige's open mouth. When her teeth caught it, she paused. A low hum escaped her mouth around the hold on the arm. "Back off slowly," he ordered. Ezra dragged the rest of the body over to Paige, who growled from the back of her throat. He ignored her and sat protectively at her side. Paige's gaze never strayed from him, and when she let out a huff, Ezra responded with his own.

I slowly released her wrists and watched Paige's arms fly up to grip the arm in her mouth. She tore off a chunk of flesh, devouring it. Any human would have been sickened by the sight, the way the blood dripped down her mouth, her chin, and even the sides of her face. Only we wouldn't be. I hunted and ate animals in my other form. Asher drank blood to live, and it was obvious what Paige did was out of necessity—a need to survive.

My brows dipped. A sudden word rolled through my mind. "I thought they were extinct," I commented quietly.

Asher gently slid out from under Paige. She snarled at being disturbed, but other than that, she didn't care. Our boss sat on the ground beside her and stared on in astonishment.

He shook his head and replied to my comment, "That was what had been told centuries ago. The council implied they were bad, too powerful, and were trying to take over all of humanity. Before I even joined the elite, the council had wiped them out as a threat."

The naked guy grunted, and all eyes trained on him.

"Who are you?" I asked roughly.

"Thorn Jones. She is under my guard."

I crossed my arms over my chest and snorted. "We can't be sure of that."

"I was sent to her magically when her change hit. It occurred after I'd showered."

Huh, that explained why the guy was butt naked. Yet, he didn't seem to care.

Shaking my head, I told him, "We need to know everything you do."

We all tensed when Thorn narrowed his eyes. His upper lip raised, and he snarled, "None of you need to know anything. I will be taking her when she is self-aware."

In a blink, Asher stood in front of him with fangs showing. His vampire had come out to play. "You'll not take her."

Thorn moved closer, not caring he faced Asher's vampire. "I will. She is not your concern."

"Listen, dickhead," Asher bit out. "You might as well say

we're the authority in this scenario, and we protect people. She looks all of seventeen, and my guess is, she doesn't know you at all. She's not going anywhere unless we deem it safe for her."

"She's twenty-five, and she *will* want to go with me."

"She's twenty-five?" Smith asked as he came to stand beside me. "She looks about sixteen."

Fuck, she really did, which was why I felt like a dick when, at first glance, I'd thought about how hot she was and how good she'd look under me.

I quickly pushed that thought aside. Even if she was of age, it didn't change the damn situation we were in.

"I think we're all getting off track here," I said snappishly. "How about we go back to her being a ghoul."

"What?" Smith yelled excitedly. "Are you serious? I mean, I can see she's eating an arm there, but it didn't cross my mind. I thought they were extinct. *This* isn't extinct." He ran his hands through his hair. He goddamn loved figuring new shit out. "Also, how is her heart beating now?"

"Asher," I called, ignoring Smith's rant. "We all agree he's not taking her until we can be assured she'll be all right and we know everything there is to know. Right?"

"Yes." Asher nodded curtly.

Paige flipped herself up to crouch over the dead body. The arm no longer holding her interest, she bent and sniffed the body. We all watched and waited.

"Do you want some clothes?" I heard Smith ask, no doubt to the naked guy who was stepping up behind Paige. She turned her head to the side and hissed. I made a move toward them, but Ezra stood and let out a warning growl.

"You move again, I'll stop you, and you won't like how I

do it," Asher clipped. He flashed to stand beside Paige, readying his body for a fight if need be.

Thorn's gaze narrowed more. "You have helped her this night, but I will fight you if I have to."

"Then be prepared to lose," I said. I barely held back my snort, wondering who the hell this fool thought he was. Asher by himself was no joking matter, but pitch the three of us elite enforcers together, and we were un-fucking-stoppable.

Thorn scoffed. "It'll not be me who loses."

"Uh, guys," Smith called.

"Do you know who we are?" Asher asked.

"I don't care. My priority is Paige, and nothing, nor no one, will stop me from keeping her safe."

"Guys."

"We can keep her safe as well. Hell, we'd do a better job than you. There's three of us after all," Asher pointed out. He was right. Whatever was going to happen to Paige—and the guy surely acted like something was going to happen—then there were three of us, and we'd have a better chance at keeping her safe if we had to. Thorn was one guy.

"She'll have her army once we get home."

I glanced to Asher. "Army?" I asked Thorn.

"Yes." Thorn nodded.

"Guys!" Smith snapped. Our attention went to him, and he pointed down at Paige. "I think she's coming to."

I darted my eyes to Paige. She swayed a little in her crouched form before resting her hands on the body to support herself. Blinking over and over, she shook her head and then closed her eyes, only to open them slowly, and her stunning dark blue eyes shone back up at me.

"You okay?" I asked roughly, annoyed I cared to even ask.

I hadn't cared about short, hot women's feelings or pain before. Alex handled that shit after a job was done because he had the patience to.

She nodded hesitantly and glanced to each side of her. When she looked behind her, she gasped and squeaked, "Penis." Next, she landed on her butt and covered her eyes with her hands. Ezra snorted, and I was sure I saw the hellhound roll his eyes before he plopped himself down right next to her.

Asher's gaze hit me, so did Smith's. They were shocked by my reaction. Hell, I was as well, but I couldn't stop the laugh that fell from my mouth.

When my teammates wouldn't quit staring, I threw my hands up and muttered, "I've laughed before."

Smith shook his head. "I can't remember when."

"Cover him in clothes," I ordered, changing the subject.

Smith nodded. With a click of his fingers, Thorn was dressed in jeans, biker boots, and a plain black tee.

"Paige," Asher called in a gentle tone as he crouched beside her, but Thorn moved in and placed his body between Asher and Paige. She caught the situation between spread fingers.

"What's going on?" she asked, dropping her hands, one to her lap and the other around Ezra's neck. She spared a glance at the blood on her before her eyes trailed to the body and arm. "I... ah, did I have a snack?" Confusion dipped her brows, and she gripped her hellhound tighter.

"You did, but something happened—"

"What?" she interrupted, her voice tight with fear.

"That's what we'd like to know." Asher smiled softly at her from around Thorn's legs.

"What do you mean?" She shook her head. "What

happened after— Where is everyone? Is my sister okay? Did something else happen? Did I black out? Is my family all right?"

Thorn laid a hand on her shoulder. "Calm. Everyone is fine."

She lifted her gaze to him. "Who in the hell are you?"

I snorted when Paige shrugged off Thorn's hand and stood. She swayed a little. Without thinking, my body moved to help steady her. She brought her eyes to mine, gave me a nod, and moved her attention back to Thorn. "Who are you?"

"I'm your protector."

Since I was still holding her arm and, somehow, my other hand had slid to her waist, I felt her tense. What I hated most was how I could scent he spoke the truth.

"My protector? What does that mean?" She searched all our faces.

"He showed after a power surge shot out of your body," I answered.

She shook her head. "A power surge?"

"I'll explain everything when we're alone and safe," Thorn told her.

I stopped the growl rising in my throat by thinning my lips. My wolf and I didn't like the fact this cocksucker kept wanting to get her alone and away.

"As we've said, you'll not be taking her until we deem it safe," Asher replied.

Paige drew her hands up and waved them in front of herself as she stepped back and out of my grip. I didn't like it. "Hold up." She shook her head. "Ezra," she called. He stood, and I was sure he gave us a smirk as he made his way to her side. Paige reached out to run her hand over his head, as if for comfort.

Fucking hell, did the hellhound smile cockily for being the one she trusted most?

I'd easily wipe if from his smug face. I clenched my fists at my sides.

"Miss Alice," Smith started, asking for her attention.

Her nose screwed up. "Paige," she told him.

He smiled, red coating his cheeks. Guess I wasn't the only one attracted to Paige, which was strange. I was sure Smith was gay. Not that I'd ask. We didn't talk about our private lives. We worked well together, and that was all that mattered. He didn't cower when I was a prick, which happened a lot since my wolf was an alpha and a bastard in his own right. Alex had only been on our team five years. He'd joined us after we'd lost our last mage in battle. A guy who thought nothing and no one was as good as him. The dick deserved to die, especially after we found out he didn't take no for an answer and beat women he'd been with. Alex was ten times better than him anyway.

Shit, we were all protective to a certain point of innocents, but there was something about Paige where I felt the need to curl her in bubble wrap, tuck her under my arm, and run from everything and everyone to keep her safe.

That shit was fucked up.

Why her?

"Paige," he muttered. "Um, I'm sure we can get things sorted. We have questions, you have them, and that guy also has them. We just need to sit down calmly and talk things out."

"I don't have questions," Thorn stated.

"You have answers we want to know before you think you can take Paige anywhere." Asher glared.

"Wait, what? I'm not going anywhere with anyone." Ezra gently bumped his head into her shoulder. "Except for Ezra."

"My queen, you need to come with me. I'm your protector. Before others know of your existence, we need to get you to your fortress."

Queen? What the fuck? The queen of what and who? This cockhead needed to explain. My wolf wanted to reach down his throat for the answers.

Her eyes widened, then quickly narrowed. "Are you high? Drunk? On *something*?"

Smith laughed. When Thorn sent a snarl his way, Smith covered his laugh by coughing. I met Asher's amused stare with one of my own.

"No, my queen—"

"Stop with the queen stuff. I'm not a queen. I'll never be one, and really, I don't think I'd want to be one."

Thorn stepped toward her, his hands out, reaching. Asher slid in front of her, and I moved back to her side. Ezra huffed out in annoyance on her other side, and Smith took her back. Thorn's brows dipped, his lips thinning.

"I would never harm her," he growled low.

"We don't know that," I said. Paige's gaze shifted to me. Her head tilted, and I could scent she was confused by me, but she also smelled of fear and skepticism.

"I would only ever protect her." Thorn fumed through clenched teeth.

When Paige cleared her throat, the others glanced at her. "This is all fun and games, but I'm tired," she lied. "I just want to go home and sleep. We can revisit this weird trip tomorrow." More lies.

"Ah...," Smith started. She shifted to meet his eyes, and another blush sprang to his cheeks. Jesus, was the boy a virgin or something? "I'm not sure if you know, but we can tell you're lying."

Her head jerked back. "Bullshit."

He shook his head, a playful smile on his lips.

"Huh." She nodded. "Right." She glanced around at all of us. "Well, I guess I'll go for the truth."

CHAPTER FIVE
ALEX

My lips wanted to twitch. Actually, I just wanted to laugh. Paige was too easy to read. The way her gaze moved around us all quickly told me she was trying to think of another way out of the situation. It wasn't only that, though. I wasn't like Nate or Asher who could taste a lie. I could feel one.

"Smith?" she asked my name.

"Alex, actually. I prefer only my teammates to call me Smith when on the job," I told her, and when she smiled softly, I knew my damn face heated. There was something about the woman that sang to my desires. I wanted to reach out and touch her, hold her, and tell her everything would be all right. I didn't though, of course. I had a feeling she'd punch me.

I could tell I wasn't the only one affected by Paige. It seemed all of our protective instincts were lit for the woman. What was it about her that caused such a reaction?

"Right, Alex." My cock jerked behind my jeans when she said my name. She ran a hand through her hair, then looked at her hand, staring at the blood and no doubt becoming aware it was smeared in her beautiful hair. She cursed under her breath. "Right, ah, where was I?"

"The truth," I offered.

She clicked her fingers and pointed at me. "Yes." She nodded and moved away to face the four of us. Ezra, the hellhound, something I still couldn't believe, followed her like a well-trained dog and allowed her to pat him on his head. He leaned into her. "The truth of the matter is... I feel"—she touched her chest—"like I can trust you all. But all of this is strange. Up until now, I've never met someone else who's different like me. It's a lot to take in, and right now, all I want is a shower and to think."

"You can do both at the castle," Thorn offered.

She threw up her hands. "I don't even know your name."

He bent at the waist. "Thorn Jones, my queen."

Paige's eyes darkened. "You call me queen one more time and my fist is going up your ass," she threatened. Thorn straightened. His lips twitched, like all of ours were because Paige was just too damn cute when she tried to be menacing. Her face blanked, and she straightened. "Wait, did you say castle?"

Another lip twitch all around. "Yes, my—" He cleared his throat. "Yes."

Paige looked at me. I didn't know why she singled me out, but I liked that she had. Her smile was radiant. "I've always wanted to see a castle."

"Then you should." I wouldn't deny her something she'd always wanted, even when Asher and Nate cursed at me. I shrugged at them. "She's always wanted to see one." I'd like to see them try and say no to her.

"Then we're accompanying her," Asher stated, crossing his arms over his chest. Thorn opened his mouth, probably to deny us, but Asher's hand shot up. "Since we work for the council on the elite enforcers team who governs the dangerous matters around the world, there isn't a chance in hell we would allow a woman to go to some castle on her own with a man she doesn't know."

Paige's eyes rounded, her mouth dropping open in surprise.

Though, what Asher had said was a crock of bullshit. It wasn't our job to escort a person somewhere. There was also the matter of how we could all sense that Thorn was speaking the truth.

"You're not allowed to accompany us. Having you know where we're situated is a risk to the queen. We don't know what your authorities would do with the information about the queen being reborn."

"Wait? Reborn?" Paige said, wide-eyed.

"Then we don't say anything," Nate growled. Everyone looked at him. "We're owed some time off. We take it now and go with them."

"I can't allow—" Thorn started.

"Wait, wait, wait," Paige called. "Can we please stop bickering? I don't understand why you all want to come, but I won't say no because I do believe none of you want to harm me, and I'm feeling Thorn thinks there'll be trouble for some reason, so it'll be safer in numbers." Her lips quickly thinned. I had a feeling she couldn't believe that she'd just said that. Unless… could she feel the same connection to us, even though it was small, like we did for her?

"Agreed," Asher said.

Thorn studied Paige, and she stared him down until he eventually sighed. "Fine."

"Finally," Paige cheered. "Now I'm closer to getting my shower."

All the men froze, and I could imagine it was because all of our minds suddenly went to the gutter and thought of Paige and her naked, sweet, soft skin in the shower.

My dick throbbed.

With a click of my fingers, Paige stood before us clean and in fresh clothes of jeans and a tee that fit snuggly across her chest. I didn't even have to bring my full power forward to be able to do that for her.

Her gaze shifted down on herself slowly. Her mouth popped open, and then she sucked in a sharp breath. Her hands patted down her chest, stomach, and thighs. She looked over at me.

"That is amazing. I won't have to shower again."

I coughed. "It's nothing really."

"Oh, it's something. I wish I could do it."

And I wished she'd stop running her hands up and down herself; it wasn't helping the situation in my jeans since my dick had a mind of its own now and wanted to come out and play with Paige. She breathed hard. She smiled hard. She ran her hands over herself... hard.

Was I the only guy having the same problem?

I glanced to the others, mainly at their crotches. Nope. I wasn't the only one with the problem. A throat cleared. I ripped my gaze up from Asher's erection and straight into his eyes. His brow raised, and my face burned.

"Hang on," Paige said, bringing our attention back to her, thankfully. The only problem was, her hands were splayed over her breast. Panic shone in her eyes. "My heart's beating." She lifted her hand to point down at her organ. "It's beating. It hasn't done that since I woke and dug my way out of the ground."

"You what?" Nate snarled. He sounded like how I felt on the inside—angered by Paige having to go through that.

She fluttered her hand Nate's way, as if saying his words didn't matter.

Instead, she asked, "What's wrong with me? Am I human

again? How? Why? Did the demon do something to me?"
This woman amazed me with how she was taking everything
in stride.

Thorn took a step forward. "We must leave this place, my
queen, but please know there is nothing wrong with you. Your
heart beats because you are Queen. I can explain more in
detail when we're safely at the castle."

She nodded, her eyes staring at her chest. "Yes. All right.
Let's go then."

"Nate, Smith, go with them while I organize our time off,"
Asher ordered. He turned to Thorn. "Are there sufficient
feeding rooms provided? If not, I will make sure I'm catered
for."

"It's strange to feel it beat after so long," Paige mumbled
to herself, still touching her chest. I kept my lips tightly
pressed together because I was close to moaning. Why did I
react this way to her?

"There will be enough provided. We have plenty of people
on the grounds. All types."

Nate snorted. "How do you know they're trustworthy?"

Thorn glared at him. "They have sworn their allegiance to
the new queen before she was created."

"Does that mean other things in my body will work?"
Paige asked, seemingly oblivious to the conversation going on
around her. Her fingers pressed against her neck. "Hey, I have
a pulse." Happiness rushed through my chest when she
smiled.

"So because they've sworn their allegiance, they won't
harm her in any way?" Nate asked with a smirk.

Thorn's jaw clenched. "If they break it, they die. They
know this."

Nate scoffed. "Sometimes money and status can talk more than a threat."

"I feel like I need to go to the bathroom," Paige said, her eyes wide with wonderment. Then they narrowed. "Does this mean I'll get my period again?"

I palmed my face. We did not need to hear about her period. It was time to intervene. I clapped and said, "How about we take this conversation out of here so I can break the barrier on the restaurant and we can get things rolling."

"How far away is this place?" Paige asked Thorn.

"We fly for four hours, my—" Paige held up her fist, and Thorn altered to "Paige."

"Is it overseas? I don't have a passport."

"You won't need one, Paige. We have our own aircraft."

Asher turned to me. "Clean it up, Smith."

I nodded and stepped back a few paces. I caught Paige's gasp when my eye color changed. A spell dropped from my lips, and all the furniture swirled up into the air, fixed itself, and moved back to where it had been.

Asher stepped up to what remained of the body and pointed down at the stained carpet. "Got it," I told him, adding it into the spell already created and activated.

Warmth touched my back, and I glanced over my shoulder to see a bug-eyed Paige there. "Hi," she said.

"Hey," I breathed and blushed. She rolled her head to the side, taking me in and looking cute. I actually wanted to press my lips against hers.

Her eyes hooded and darkened. "Do you know you smell wonderful?"

Holy motherchuck. What was going on? I didn't know, but I wanted to know badly. Only I couldn't because it would be a distraction. My cock strained in my jeans when her hands touched my waist and sent a zap throughout me. My heart ate at my ribs; it felt like it wanted out of my body to get to her.

What the hell?

"Nate," I called with a strained voice.

If it had been a short spell, I wouldn't have needed so much focus, but there'd been damage all over the place, even outside when Nate and the hellhound were at each other.

I caught Nate moving close, but then Paige shook her head and blinked. She said, "That's really damn cool how you do that. Your eyes are... wow."

I cleared my throat, then swirled my tongue around because it was suddenly dry. "Ah, thanks."

She stepped back, smiling. "I better go to the bathroom in case.... What a night, right?"

"Definitely different," I replied with my own smile. She turned and walked off toward the bathroom with Ezra following. Of course I watched her go, and I knew the other guys would be as well. Once she was through the door, with the hellhound standing outside of it glaring at us, I asked, "I'm not the only one feeling this pull toward her, right?"

"No," Asher said.

"Fuck. No," Nate replied, anger ever present in his tone. He was always pissed though, so I didn't wonder why he'd be angry about this.

"It shouldn't have happened," Thorn mumbled. All our gazes locked onto him.

"What do you mean?" I asked as the final chair slid into place. The spell was done.

He shook his head. "We need to get to the castle. I'll explain it all there."

"You can't just throw that out and not say shit," Nate clipped.

"Nate," Asher called. He shook his head and gestured toward the bathroom. Meaning Paige was probably listening in and he didn't think she'd want or need to know what Thorn meant just yet. She'd been through enough for one night.

Nate's jaw clenched, his hands fisting in frustration. Still, he nodded. The bathroom door opened, and Paige stepped out, saw all of us looking at her, and rolled her eyes. "So I don't need to use the bathroom still. But I was sure I needed to pee." She shrugged. "I can't figure it out."

"All will be answered soon, Paige," Thorn said.

"I know." She sighed. "Look, I need to check on my sister before we go anywhere. She'll freak if she can't contact me."

I glanced to Thorn. "Nate and I could take Paige and meet you at the airport," I suggested. Thorn seemed wary, but after looking at Paige, he finally agreed, stating he had things to prepare for our departure. He also probably knew he wouldn't get Paige to go if he didn't give her this.

"Come on then," Nate said and started for the door.

"I'll be in contact," Asher announced, and using his speed, he took the body and left the room.

Paige tried to track his movements, but it would be impossible. She then glanced to Thorn. "Thank you, and we won't be long. I just need to let her know I'll be safe."

"I understand." He bowed again before straightening. Paige and her hellhound, who was back in his canine form, followed Nate out while I hung back because Thorn's gaze came to me. "You'll have an hour. It's too risky for anything longer. Others may feel her power. Be at hanger twenty by then."

"We will."

"Be sure to keep her safe."

"You have my word."

He opened his mouth as if to say more, but then shook his head. As he went toward the back area, I made my way outside where Nate was already in the driver seat. Paige sat in the back with her hellhound.

I took the passenger seat in the front, even though I wanted to squeeze into the back with Paige. I didn't think the hellhound would appreciate it.

"Address?" Nate barked. He was probably still pissy because he'd laughed.

Paige rattled off the address. Nate started the car and pulled out onto the road. I wanted to turn around and say something, anything to get her attention, but I sat still like a moron, unsure what the best thing would be to say.

Never had I expected the night would lead us to be in a car with a woman who had somehow dug her claws into us. It was also something she'd never foreseen, but it had me wondering. Did she feel a connection to us?

CHAPTER SIX
PAIGE

I didn't know if this was one big, fat wet dream or not. I had to get real with myself. I knew supernatural people were out there; I was one of them for crying out loud. But seriously, had my mind conjured up four stunningly hot males and I was living out a fantasy? Not that I had a fantasy about four men at once. And if asked, I would deny, deny, deny.

So really, it was either a dream or I was tripping big-time.

Did Ezra spike my drink with an LSD?

I glanced at Ezra. He sat with his head hanging out the window, tongue lolled out to the side having the time of his life.

I quickly pinched myself.

Okay, it wasn't a dream.

Which meant everything that had happened did, well... happen.

It all felt normal until I woke. It wasn't the sight of a dick staring me in the face that changed me. It was when I realized I had a heartbeat, a pulse. It was the fact I sensed I could trust the men around me. I didn't even know them, but deep within, there was a connection to them that I couldn't even begin to explain, let alone understand. And it started when I'd first saw them but deepened more once I knew they'd had my back in there. It was strange.

Then, when Alex used his magic, something came over

me. I wanted to reach out to him, touch him... even lick him, nip at him, kiss him, and fuck him. Raw power shot to my stomach and groin.

It was something I had never felt before.

Which was why I'd fought it and used the excuse of going to the bathroom to see if I needed to pee. I hadn't, but I wanted time away to calm myself.

I still wanted to reach into the front of the car and rub my hands all over him. I even had a thought to sniff him. He, like all of them, was stunning.

Even Thorn.

Thorn who'd showed up after my power surge apparently. Whatever that meant.

If I didn't need answers, I would be running for the hills because my connection to them scared my panties off. I hoped my emotions were well hidden. I didn't want them to know they'd affected me so deeply, just in case I did have to run.

Alex cleared his throat. "Do you know what you are?" he asked, turning in his seat to look at me. I quickly sat on my hands, so they didn't betray me and grab him. It took every ounce of willpower to not haul him into the back seat with me.

I cleared my throat, not used to my heart's rhythm, and it liked Alex a whole lot, beating wildly at the sight of him. "Um, sort of, I think." He waited for me to continue. I didn't want to give my answer in case I was wrong and looked like a fool. However, I got lost staring into his soft gray eyes. Blue eyes that turned purple. I squeezed my legs together. Nate picked that moment to draw in the air; he shot me a dirty look in the rearview mirror. I gave him one back.

"Paige?" Alex said.

I shifted my gaze to his. "A ghoul."

Alex smiled. I sucked in a deep breath because I wanted to wipe that smile away with my own lips. He nodded. "That's right."

Gripping the seat, I added, "But I have a heartbeat now, so does that make me different again?"

"We're here," Nate clipped, which he seemed to do a lot. I had a feeling it was just his nature, but I worried it'd cause us to butt heads in time because I wouldn't take his shit. He pulled up out front of my sister's house and climbed out.

"Hey," Alex said, gaining my attention. "We don't know if it has changed you, but we'll find the answers out soon, and together."

Would kissing him really be out of the question?

Probably, so instead, I gave him a smile. Immediately, a blush spread across his cheeks. Maybe I wasn't the only one feeling this. "Thank you, Alex."

He nodded and quickly exited the car.

Ezra let out a huff. The dirty dog sniffed at my crotch and shot me a knowing look. I pushed him away. "You dick. It's not like I can help it. My body just reacts."

He let out a wheeze that sounded like a laugh. Grumbling, I opened my door. Ezra jumped over me and out, landing perfectly on all fours. I got out slowly, thinking about what I would tell my sister. *"It's all right, Yasmin. I don't know them, but they set something off inside me where I know I can trust them, so I'm going with them. Also, my body seems to react to them in a carnal way."* Yeah, I wasn't sure that would work, but maybe if I told her what I'd figured out and how I needed answers, she would understand.

I walked up the path to her front door. Ezra was at my side, and I knew Nate was at my back, with Alex just behind him. "What can I tell her?" I asked.

"She's your blood, so anything as long as you know she'll not say anything to anyone," Alex replied.

"Unless you want to keep them safe. If so, say nothing," Nate added like an ass. But at least he was truthful. Would people come after Yasmin because of me? I didn't know, and I didn't want to risk it. But I also knew if the shoe were on the other foot, I'd want to know everything no matter what. She'd already seen my strength and speed when Oscar started to fall off a ladder. I'd gotten to him quickly, so he wouldn't hit the ground, taking his weight like it wasn't a problem for me. After her shock, she questioned me again and again, but in the end, she believed me when I told her I didn't have all the answers, but when I did, I promised her I would tell her. So really, I couldn't go back on that.

Before I could knock, the door swung open and Yasmin stood in it wearing winter pajamas with pigs all over it. "What's going on?" Her gaze flicked behind me. "Have you been arrested?"

Rolling my eyes, I asked, "Why do you think I've been arrested?"

"Because there're two men following you and they look professional."

My face screwed up. I stopped in the doorway and glanced behind me. I supposed they did look professional. I looked back at my sister. "Well, I'm not arrested."

She leaned in and whispered, "Are they from an asylum? I can vouch you're not crazy. They might believe me if they don't ask too many questions."

A muffled laugh sounded behind me. I knew it was Nate and his super hearing. "Yasmin, it's fine. Let's go inside and I'll explain. Are the kids in bed?"

"Yes." She stepped back and let us all in. Ezra made a

beeline for the kids' room until Yasmin snapped, "Stop." Ezra glared over his shoulder at my sister. "If you go in there and wake them up, you have to stay the night to take care of them."

Ezra glanced up to me, then back to Yasmin. He huffed, turned, and walked back our way. Passing Yasmin, he let out a growl.

"I swear your dog is too smart to be normal."

A laugh escaped me. "Yeah."

We followed Yasmin into the living room. Eric was sitting on the couch but stood when we entered, taking us all in before his gaze snapped back to me. "What have you done now?"

I threw my hands in the air. "Why do you both think I've done something? Can't I just come to my sister's house with men you don't know and it be normal?"

"No," they said together.

"Fine, it's not, but still one day it will be. So stop assuming." I took a seat on the couch beside theirs. "However, I haven't done anything wrong." Ezra climbed onto the couch and plonked himself next to me, his head landing on my lap. I pat him absently, noticing Alex and Nate didn't sit; they chose to stand behind me, which was weird. I watched Eric's and Yasmin's gaze ping-pong back and forth between us all.

"Just introduce us and tell us what all this is about," Yasmin demanded.

"Do you need money?" Eric asked.

I scoffed. "No."

"Are they threatening you in any—"

Yasmin's hand slapped down on Eric's thigh. "Honey, how about we wait and see what all this is about?" It wasn't until I looked back at Alex and then Nate, who was glowering at Eric, that I realized why Yasmin interrupted.

Eric nodded.

Ezra groaned and rolled onto his back. I absently ran my hand up and down his chest. I'd decided to go for the truth. "Okay. Here's the thing. First, this here is Nate and Alex. Second, you know I've been different for a while, right?" Yasmin and Eric nodded. "Apparently I got changed into a ghoul somehow." Their faces morphed into ones of humor. My hand came up, hoping they'd hold off laughing. They did, so I went on, "Third. Tonight, I rocked up to the restaurant you were at for Eric's promotion."

I glanced at Alex. "Do they remember that?" He shook his head. "Right." I nodded and sent Yasmin and Eric a grimace, then an apology smile. "All right. It might be harder to believe because you guys don't remember, but you and all the other patrons in the place were being held hostage by a demon. I came in, saved the day, but then something happened to me. I passed out, and when I woke, my heart's beating again, so I don't know if I've changed again. Thorn, who magically appeared in the restaurant after I passed out, tells me I'm a Queen, with a capital Q, and that I need to get to the safety of my castle where he'll answer all my questions. Asher, the boss of their group"—I thumbed behind me—"Nate, and Alex are tagging along to find out the answers as well because they don't trust Thorn."

They blinked slowly at me.

Yasmin patted Eric's thigh before she stood. "I'll start packing."

I shoved Ezra off me and also stood. "Wait, what?"

"Do you seriously think you can leave with men you don't

know without me?" She threw a hand out. "They could be murderers for all we know."

It was my turn to blink slowly. "You believe me?"

Eric stood beside his wife, placing an arm around her shoulders. "Of course your sister does." Out of the corner of his mouth, he muttered, "Right?"

She elbowed him. "Yes! I know my sister, and I know when something's happened to her. You're stronger, faster, and I'm not sure you know this, but there's something up with your dog. I didn't know about the heartbeat part, but if you think you're a ghoul, then I'm not going to argue with you. I want answers as much as you do. We'll find them together."

My new heart skipped over a beat, and my eyes misted. I hadn't cried in forever because I couldn't shed a tear. It seemed, along with my heart, that had changed also.

I walked to my sister, shoved Eric out of the way, and hugged her tightly to me.

"Too much." She breathed the words out. I released my hold a little, then pulled back and shook her with my hands on her shoulders.

"You believe me."

"I believe you. To some extent."

"We wouldn't harm her. You don't have to travel with us," Alex said.

Yasmin was already shaking her head. "I'm coming. Eric, wake the kids and get your things ready."

"Hang on, *everyone*?" I asked.

"Yes, everyone," Eric stated.

"You're not dealing with life-altering situations without your family at your back."

"But Eric just got a promotion."

We both looked at him. He shrugged. "I can find another

job. What I won't find is another wife. I go where Yasmin goes."

"But the kids—"

"They're coming," Yasmin informed.

A throat cleared, and we all faced Nate. "They'll see things that aren't normal."

"Their aunt isn't normal. They'll face it sooner or later. It just happens to be sooner." I wasn't sure if Yasmin was thinking clearly. She was being my older protective sister, and I loved her for it. But her family, her husband, and kids were important. I didn't want them risked because she felt it was her sisterly duty to help me.

"Their lives will be changed forever with the knowledge they find," Alex added.

Yasmin looked at Eric. They somehow silently conversed before tears brimmed in her eyes. "I'm rushing into things again."

I rubbed my hands up and down her arms. "You are, and it's always been in your nature to protect me. I don't need it, Yasmin. I can take care of myself. You don't have to uproot your lives for me."

She shook her head. "I can't have you not around. The kids will miss their crazy aunt. I'll miss my sister."

"And I'll be back to see you all. I just don't know when."

A knock sounded on the front door. Spinning around, I pushed Yasmin behind me. Ezra climbed to his feet, growling. Nate lifted his head and sniffed the air. "Shifter. Feline," he snarled.

A voiced shouted through the door. "Hello? It's May. Can I come in?"

"It's our neighbor," Eric said. He started for the door, but I grabbed his arm, shaking my head. I'd met twenty-year-old

May before, but I'd never sensed anything from her. I hadn't known she was a shifter, but the question was if she was going to be trouble or not.

I looked to Nate and Alex. "Is she a threat?" I whispered. They shrugged.

The door opened and May slipped in. She quickly closed it and leaned against it. "You need to leave. Now. All of you. Demons are on the way." Her eyes locked on mine. "Your power is calling to them."

Nate stepped closer to her. "How do you know this?"

"I was on my way home when I caught a group of them. I overheard them saying just that and how they're planning to storm this house to get to her."

Over my shoulder, I told Yasmin. "Get the kids and anything important you need. Make sure they're dressed warm and be quick." Her eyes shone with fear, but she nodded and ran from the room with Eric following.

My stupid heart beat so fast it caused my ears to ring. I'd brought trouble to my sister's doorstep, and now she didn't have a choice but to run with us... if we could make it out.

CHAPTER SEVEN
PAIGE

Ezra strode to my side still in his dog form. He headbutted my leg and whined. I ran my hand over his head; it calmed me a little.

I looked to the others. "Will we make it out?" I asked with a quiver to my voice. They didn't say anything, and it didn't bode well, having them unsure.

"I'll call Asher," Alex said.

"No. We'll leave now and outrun them to the airport," Nate clipped. "We have enough strength between us." He focussed on Alex.

I faced May, who'd been looking at Alex in a way I really didn't like. "Hey," I called rather harshly. Her eyes shot to me. "Why did you warn us?"

"I've been under a demon's rule. I'd never want that for another."

"You'll have to come with us," Alex said, and I hated he had. "They may have seen her come in, and if they see her leave, they'll gun for her."

May looked back to Alex with an appreciative smile. It rolled my stomach.

"Where can we dump her?" I asked and then slapped a hand over my mouth while everyone looked at me strangely. "Sorry, that, uh, came out wrong."

What was wrong with me?

Really, I should have been freaking out about demons overrunning us, wanting to kidnap me for my power, whatever that meant. Instead, I worried Alex would enjoy May's attention. It was messed up.

Wait… why would the demons be out there waiting for us to come out? Why didn't they just attack?

I voiced my confusion. Nate and Alex shared a look. May took a step closer. "I know, I don't understand it myself, but I do know we'll have to risk it to get out."

"Lies," Nate growled.

May glared at Nate, "Shut it, dog."

Ezra growled low and took a step closer to May. "I don't think he likes you," I told her.

May jutted her hand out. Long, spiky claws grew. "I'll slice him open if he comes closer," she snarled.

"What happened to the nice, helpful May?" I asked.

"Nate," Alex said. Nate shook his head. "I have to."

All of a sudden, May ran at Alex. I yelled, "Ezra." He gave chase. May bounced off something in front of Alex and fell to the floor. Ezra stood close and started pacing back and forth in front of her.

"Do not fucking move," I bit out. May sneered up at me but didn't move. I wasn't above having Ezra ripping out her throat. I didn't like her going for Alex one single bit.

"What do you want with Alex?" I demanded.

May said nothing.

Yasmin and Eric raced into the room, a child in each of their arms, a bag slung over their shoulders. "What's going on?" Yasmin asked. "May, what are you doing on the floor?"

"Aunty Paige," Sophie cried. My six-year-old niece waved wildly at me while Oscar, my eight-year-old nephew in his dad's arms, took in the room silently.

"Hey, pumpkin." I waved back. "Hiya, little dude." I winked at Oscar. "May just had a fall. We don't want her to get up in case she hurt herself."

"Alex," Nate clipped. The kid's eyes turned on him and widened. I caught Alex's eyes change to purple, and my knees wobbled a little while my clit throbbed.

So not the time, body.

Nate's gaze shot to me and turned judgy.

"Hi, guys, my name's Alex, and I'm a friend of your aunt's."

Ignoring all the silent accusations in not only Nate's eyes but Ezra's, and even May's, I faced Alex, who had his back to me while he stood in front of my family.

"Your eyes are real pretty," Sophie whispered.

My chest burned in jealousy.

What the high waters was wrong with me?

"Thank you, sweetheart. I'm going to show you something. Look at my hands." When they did, I heard a click, as if Alex snapped his fingers, and I saw the kids' eyes close. Their heads fell back into their parents' shoulders. Alex straightened. "They'll sleep for a while."

"Thank you," Yasmin said with a smile, and I would not think of punching it off her face. I wouldn't.

"Now, let's throw this ho out of the house and get out of here," I suggested.

"What did May do?" Eric asked.

"She's with the demons outside," Alex explained.

"We can't," Nate said from the window. "They have the house surrounded." He stepped back and glanced to Alex. Then he nodded before gesturing to May. "You need to leave."

She glared up at him. "They'll find you. They won't stop

until they have her." She leaped up, arms outstretched toward me. I heard Yasmin cry out as I braced, ready for her attack, but then Ezra was there. His body shook and morphed as his jaw circled her neck. The audible snap echoed in the otherwise still room.

Ezra dropped to the floor with May's neck and shoulder still in his mouth. We all watched as he released his grip and she fell to the floor, lifeless.

"Well, there goes that problem," I said. Everyone looked at me with widened eyes. I realized it sounded heartless, but I couldn't bring forth two fucks to give. I shrugged. "I'm sorry, but it was going to be her or me. I'm glad it was her. Good job, Ezra," I said, and I was sure he preened under my appraisal. "And let's not forget she was with the demons that are after me."

Nate snorted and shook his head, but I was sure I saw his mouth twitching. "We better get the fuck outta here."

"My way," Alex stated.

Nate shook his head. "No."

"Nate, we don't have a choice."

"You'll be knocked out from it."

"What's this?" I asked, glancing to my sister and her husband to see if they had an idea, but their eyes were glued to Ezra, who sat licking around his mouth. "Oh, yeah. I forgot to mention. Ezra's a hellhound. I found that out tonight too. I mean, I knew he was different, just not in what way."

"A hellhound?" Eric murmured.

"Yes."

"A hellhound was around our children?" Yasmin screeched, causing us to flinch. "They climbed over a hellhound?"

"Um... yes?"

"H-He just killed May."

"Ah, I didn't think you two were close?" I asked.

Yasmin shook her head. She seemed a little pale, but she was managing, like Eric. "We weren't. She kept on flirting with Eric. I never trusted her, but... death?"

"It's gonna come down to them or us," Nate said gruffly. Something crashed outside. Nate swore. He nodded to Alex, and then Alex called, "Everyone gather around me." His eyes bled to purple, and I was the first one to him, sliding my arms around his waist. His eyes bugged out as he looked down at me. His cheeks flamed with heat as he coughed and said, "Ah, yes, so, uh, grab onto me somehow. Nate, take hold of Ezra." Nate cursed, and I heard Ezra growl.

"Yasmin? Eric?"

"We're here and ready," Eric said.

The front door was blown open, and long-legged things crawled through the opening. Alex started chanting, and suddenly, a wind from nowhere picked up around us. Yasmin whimpered behind me. I reached my free arm out and gripped her to me.

As a white light shone through the room, I screwed my eyes closed, and then there was nothing but a tingle over my body. I opened my eyes in time to see Alex crumple and fall from my grip to the floor.

"Alex," I cried, dropping to my knees. Terrified, I rested a hand on his arm and chest. He was breathing.

"My queen," a voice came from beside me. Then arms circled around Alex, ready to drag him from my grip.

"No," I snarled and shoved the person away. They flew out to the side, slamming into the side of the plane and falling to the ground in a heap.

"Paige" was called roughly. I glanced up to see Thorn approaching. "What's wrong? What happened?"

I got to my hands and hovered over Alex's body, protecting him. He'd used his magic to get us out of there, but something had happened to him because of it. "Stop," I ordered, my voice cold and hard.

A breeze blew across my face, and then Asher stood in front of me, facing Thorn. "What happened?" His voice was hard. He glanced behind him and down at us. I caught the sight of his elongated teeth and vibrant, glowing green eyes. My body quivered.

No. Not now. Jesus, Paige, get a grip.

Men rushed at us. Asher snarled at them.

"Fuck's sake, stop," Nate called. He stood off to the side with Ezra sitting beside him.

"Stop," Thorn repeated, and the men did.

"Everyone cool it. No one here is going to harm anyone," Nate said, and then he waved a hand at me. "She overreacted. Didn't know Smith would pass out from teleporting a group of us. She panicked."

I cocked my head to the side. "Alex passed out? He's okay?" Relief washed through me, along with a mild case of embarrassment. Though I would totally do it again if it came down to protecting him. Strange, and yet it felt natural.

Nate snorted. "He's fine. Well, he will be. He's good to travel with one person, maybe two. More exhausts him."

Asher straightened, fixing his clothes before stepping up to our sides. I moved back to kneel beside Alex. My body settled, knowing Alex would be okay. Asher bent, picked Alex up in his arms, and started for the plane. I quickly got up, raced toward them, and grabbed Alex's hand. I couldn't leave his side just yet, not until I knew for certain he was okay. Asher glanced down at me and then forward. I wanted to bring his face down to mine. I wanted him to bring those pointy teeth out so I could lick them, suck them while his glowing eyes gazed into mine.

Wetness pooled between my legs. I ground my teeth together, and someone groaned behind us. Asher looked back down at me with surprise in his eyes. His step faltered for a fraction of a second before they smoothed out as if it didn't happen. A tick in his jaw told me that misstep annoyed him. He climbed the stairs with me close behind, my hand still clutching Alex's. Ezra, who'd at some time changed back into his canine form, let out a huff and came up behind me.

Whispers brushed by my ears, but I didn't take them in. Since I knew things were safer, I rested all my concentration on those close around me because my mind was already too full.

Then I remembered something at the top of the stairs and turned. "Yasmin," I called. How I forgot I didn't know, and guilt threaded through me.

She still stood where we'd teleported in. "He… you… the man… oh my God," she exclaimed and then stormed my way.

People I didn't know went to step in her way, until I called, "She's my sister. No one touches her." They moved back. Asher stepped inside the plane. I quickly followed with my hand still in Alex's. Since I knew Yasmin would catch up and that she'd be safe because it seemed the people around us listened to what I said, I didn't worry.

I released my hold on Alex when Asher lay him in a seat near the window. Then I sat next to Alex, taking his hand again. Asher shot me a puzzled look and sat across from us in another seat. Ezra plonked his backside next to me in the aisle —thankfully they were wide. Thorn, followed by Nate, entered before my sister and Eric barreled in. Nate sat next to Asher while Thorn took a seat opposite us. Yasmin and Eric, still holding the kids, sat in the group of four chairs with Thorn.

Other people climbed aboard. I noticed the man I'd thrown. When he looked at me, I said, "I'm sorry for throwing you."

He bowed. "I'm sorry for touching him, my queen." Before I could correct him on the queen part, he moved down the aisle.

Yasmin turned to me. "I knew you were strong, but not that strong. He shot straight over. I'm surprised the plane isn't dented. Then"—she leaned in to me—"his"—she gestured with her head Asher's way—"eyes glowed green, his teeth... did you see his teeth?" I nodded. Boy had I seen his teeth. "Who are these guys, Paige?" She looked down at my hand in Alex's.

I cleared my throat. It was going to sound weird no matter how I said it, so I just went for it. "You see, I met them tonight. Alex and Nate you already know. But what you don't know is that Alex is a mage. Nate is a shifter. Asher is a vampire, and Thorn is..." I stumbled a moment. "What are you?"

"A ghoul, like yourself."

My heart skipped a beat.

"Ah... right, there you go."

"Psst," my sister whispered, leaning in again. Rolling my eyes, I looked to her. "It doesn't explain that." Again she stared down at my hand.

"No, it doesn't because I can't really explain it myself. I just know I don't want to leave his side until he's awake and okay. It's freaking me out on the inside though."

Yasmin nodded. "I can see the crazy eyes coming out to play." Yes, she knew me well. I may not show how freaked I was, but on the inside, I cursed, sweated, curled into a ball, and sucked my thumb. The night was all too much and soon, if it didn't slow down—and I worried it wouldn't—I *would* be in a corner legit sucking my thumb and crying for a blanket.

"Also," I added to Yasmin, "there's no point in whispering. They hear everything." I drew the last words out like I was telling her a scary story.

She paled. "Right. Got it. Girl talk later in private."

The men chuckled. Except for Nate. Still, his lips were going crazy. I knew he was holding back.

"Does someone want to inform me what happened?" Asher asked.

"I'd also like to know," Thorn said.

"Can we take off first?" Nate mentioned. "Probably safer if we get away fast."

"I'll speak with the pilot." Thorn stood and stalked down the aisle.

I turned in my seat to check on Alex; he breathed easy. I shifted closer, and his warmth washed over me. I wished I could curl into it, but that would bring more questions from everyone, and I didn't have an answer to them. All I knew was that Alex sent my hormones alight the first time he used his power, and since then, I'd felt a sense of protectiveness and possessiveness toward him.

Out the corner of my eye, I saw Asher studying me with Alex. He was also on my list that sent my lady bits and organs crazy. Only I noticed, like with Alex, it had started when he'd first showed his power. His vampire side.

What was wrong with me?

Did it mean I'd be after every man if they had a power or a different side to them and used it in front of me?

I'd been with one man in the past. One man who'd been a dickhead in the end, but I'd been happy having just one guy. Then bam, all of a sudden I'd changed once more and was a horny slut.

Even worse, they could smell it.

Embarrassed didn't come close to describing how I felt.

Would I have to buy a chastity belt for myself, lock it, and then throw away the key?

I checked on Yasmin and Eric to drag my mind away from thinking of a straitjacket for myself. At least then I'd keep my hands to myself. They huddled together, holding their children. Regret for going to their place muddled my head. If I hadn't have shown, they wouldn't have needed to leave their house. They'd be safe. Free. Now they were mixed up in a world I was still learning to deal with myself.

Yasmin glanced at me. "Don't," she said. "I'm not sad or angry I'm here with you. We're family."

"But—"

She shook her head. "No buts, Paige. I have no regrets."

It wasn't the place to have this conversation, but I didn't hold back because of the people around us. "I do. I should have called you, not come by. Then you'd still be home, and your kids would still be safe in their beds. Eric would have gone to his job on Monday in his new position. It wasn't fair of me—"

"Paige, my life wouldn't be the same without you in it. We've already lost our parents. I can't lose you too. Family always." She smiled.

My chest swelled. "You're the best sister ever."

Her smile grew. "I know."

"And you have the best husband." I winked at Eric. He returned it with a grin. I thought I heard a sound across from me, but when I looked in the direction, both Nate and Asher were just watching me.

The door to the cockpit opened, then over the intercom came the announcement to prepare for takeoff. I heard seat belts click in, so I did mine up as Thorn sat down in his seat.

When the plane started moving down the airstrip, Thorn said, "Now, let's talk about what happened."

CHAPTER EIGHT
PAIGE

It was Nate who explained what happened at Yasmin and Eric's. By the end of it, we were high in the sky, and a frown marred Asher's and Thorn's lips. But it was Thorn who said, "I never should have left your side, my queen."

I shot him a look, annoyed at his "my queen" business, but chose to say, "It's not anyone's fault but my own."

He shook his head. "I knew you would be sensed, but I didn't realize how fast."

"What's done is done. There is no going back now," Asher said.

"I guess you got us time off?" Nate asked.

Asher nodded. "Yes."

Nate whistled. "How did you manage that?"

"They owed us."

"Bullshit. It's because Jessica wants in your pants."

My belly sank, twisted, and then it wanted to crawl up my chest. "Who's Jessica?" I demanded harshly.

All eyes turned to me. I caught Thorn's lips thinning, his brows dipping.

"Sorry?" Asher asked.

"Who is Jessica?"

"She's a member of the council, the one in charge of our group," Nate supplied, and there went his lips again. I wanted to rip them off. I didn't find my weird aggression funny.

Humming under my breath, I turned into Alex and looked out the window. Maybe I just needed some sleep. After all, it had been an eventful evening.

"We'll speak of everything once we land and we're in private," Thorn abruptly said.

I glanced to him and asked a question I'd been wondering just before. "So you can't say why this plane was strategically planned to be ready for tonight? How did you know something would happen tonight?"

"That I can tell you." Thorn smiled, and my heart fluttered. No, not him too. But I didn't feel the need to pee on his leg like I did with Alex and Asher. However, I wouldn't be surprised if it came sooner or later. I did feel a small connection to him. I could definitely trust him. I knew that. "From our former queen. We knew a rough time of the year to be prepared for your arrival. For the last couple of weeks, we've been ready. When our queen passed, a spell drew me to your side immediately. It happened to be after a shower at the time."

It was the truth. I sensed it.

Sometimes my new senses, or power—whatever—were really handy.

It still left me with more questions, but I held off on those and moved onto something else. With a quick glance around, I lowered my voice and leaned toward Thorn's way to ask, "Ghouls... what exactly can we do?"

He smiled. "From what I've gathered, your... dog has been around since you woke." I nodded and also noted he didn't refer to Ezra as a hellhound. I assumed in case the others in the back were listening and he didn't want them to know. "He has good instincts. Did he help?"

"Yes."

"So you would know by now what you need to eat." I nodded; he returned it. "Ghouls are strong, fast, and live forever, unless our heads are sliced from our bodies." Ezra let out a growl, and I reached down and patted him. Both Ezra and I didn't like to hear it, but it was information I needed to know. "With you being the queen, you'll have more strength and speed. Really, you'll be an unstoppable force."

An unstoppable force. I liked the idea of that. It meant I could protect my family more.

"Thank you," I told him. It was all the information I needed for that moment as there were too many ears for more.

"Anything," he replied.

Shifting in my seat, I looked behind us to the seats further back. I didn't know the other people on the plane. Even if they were called "my" people, I didn't trust them. Some looked at me in awe. Others I couldn't read whether they didn't like me being here or if they were just not showing anything until I proved myself somehow.

In total, there were seven other people I didn't know. Four men and three women. The man I'd pushed smiled at me. It was the women I wasn't sure about. One even looked like she sucked on a lemon as she stared back. But then her gaze flicked to Thorn and back to me. I got it; she wanted Thorn. There went that buzz of annoyance again. That pull. Her wanting Thorn didn't sit well with me.

I faced the front, but Asher's eyes met mine, looking into my soul. Unable to process everything, I rested my head against Alex's shoulder and closed my eyes. I did feel tired, but I was too wired to fall asleep. Instead, I listened to Yasmin and Eric talking about what they were going to tell the kids when they woke. Then I heard Nate calling for Asher's attention. They spoke about the demon in the restaurant, how it was a weak one, but there'd been more and more popping up over town.

It was listening to them all that surprisingly lulled me into sleep.

* * *

"She's been holding my hand the whole way?" Alex's voice drifted into my sleep, causing me to shiver. He was okay.

"Yep." Nate popped the *p* at the end.

"Why?" he asked. He didn't seem too fazed by it. He was still holding my hand. That was a good sign, right? He might be okay with me wrapping him in bubble wrap to keep him safe.

Wait... throw that thought out of my head; it was insane.

As I opened my eyes, I realized no sound was coming from the plane. We'd landed. I straightened in the seat and hoped I hadn't drooled. Discreetly, I wiped the side of my mouth on my shoulder, just in case.

"So, we're here." Being on the ground meant I had to release Alex's hand. I slowly unstuck one finger at a time from my vise grip as Thorn explained we'd landed on "our" own private airstrip. Apparently, the former queen, not that I was admitting to being the new one, had been rich.

Without looking at Alex, I moved my hand away from his and fisted it tightly at my side as I stood and stretched.

I pulled my gaze back down and caught four men watching me intently. A smirk played on my lips. They'd been checking me out.

The people from the back of the plane started down the

aisle. They moved by, and each one bowed at me as they did. Only a couple of the women didn't bend far, and they kept their gaze on me with a slight glare in their eyes.

When I'd begun to stupidly curtsy with the first person, Thorn shook his head at me, and Asher stood, taking my arm and holding me up. Okay, so that had been wrong. The rest I felt like a fool just standing there as they bent at their waist in front of me.

When the last one left the cabin, Yasmin laughed her ass off. "They b-bowed to you." She tapped herself. "My sister."

"Shut up," I mumbled. If I wasn't weirded out, then I'd probably be laughing along with her.

Thorn stood. "Let's get you inside, my queen."

"Thorn," I warned.

"In private I will call you Paige. In public, it's better to show my allegiance and respect."

I sighed, a normal human reaction I still held. "Fine." I stilled and felt heat at my back. With a breath in, I knew it was Alex.

"What's wrong?" he asked.

If I could, I would have melted against him, but it seemed my emotions were catching up and mixing with my mind. Everything had changed. Again.

File it away, Paige. Have a breakdown in private.

I cleared my throat. "Nothing."

Yasmin gave me a sad, soft smile. She knew I was on the verge of crashing into a heap and not wanting to know more. More meant my brain would probably melt inside my head.

"Let us get you inside," Thorn said gently.

Nodding, I moved into the aisle. Ezra rose with a groan. His head thumped into my hand, and I patted him. Thorn started toward the door, and I gestured to Yasmin and Eric. They rose with the kids and moved into the space before me. I followed them, Ezra at my side, knowing the other men in our little group wouldn't be far behind.

Outside the plane, more people, at least over two hundred, stood gazing up at us. Thorn moved my family gently aside, and when the people saw me, they bowed, and all of them called, "My queen."

A tingle started in my lower spine and then spread all the way up. I straightened and tipped my head down slightly. The people went about whatever they had been doing. A lot kept glancing my way, but they still got busy.

"Well done," Thorn murmured.

I snorted softly. "What, for not freaking out?"

He smiled. "Yes."

I harrumphed and then shrugged. Glancing away from him to the opposite side, my jaw dropped open, my eyes widening. "Holy crap…. Yasmin?"

"I see it," she said, and I could tell she was smiling. Before Yasmin met Eric, we'd been planning to travel, to see the world and all the old castles we could.

Finally, I had one right in front of me, and it looked like the mother of all castles.

My chest filled with elation and warmed me all over. "It's so big," I whispered.

"That's what she said" came from Eric, who then huffed out a breath, and I knew it was from Yasmin elbowing him.

"Welcome home, my queen," Thorn said, stepping up to my side and ignoring Ezra's growl.

Home was definitely a castle.

It looked to be about the size of an extra-large football

stadium long and at least five-stories high. But there were peaks all over the place, like little bell towers. My hands itched to explore the whole place, but I knew it would take me ages, maybe even a year, to see everything. There was even a moat out the front with a raised drawbridge.

A giddy light laugh dropped from my lips.

I would get to see inside a castle.

A *castle*.

My castle apparently.

At least I had the time on my hands to explore the whole place. That was unless I didn't like the answers I was hoping to get as soon as we settled. But still, I could stay a little longer. I hadn't had an adventure like this in... ever.

With a new spring in my step, I started down the stairs. At the bottom, I took another glance toward the castle, until Ezra growled at my side. I looked down at him and then over to the woods off the airstrip. Ezra took a step that way.

"Ezra," I called.

"Paige, stop." Nate's voice was strong and hard.

In the next second, I was surrounded by Asher, Nate, Thorn, and Ezra, who'd crept back closer to my side. Behind me, near the plane, Alex stood with my family, and I shot him an appreciative smile. He dipped his chin.

"Don't take another fucking step," Nate snarled.

Facing forward, I peeked over his shoulder and saw about twenty men and woman of all shapes and sizes step from the woods. There were also wolves. At least fifty of them.

"Is she the new queen?" a man called. He was older, with gray tinting the sides of his dark hair. Built bigger than my men.

Hold up, my men?

Since when did they become my men?

Did I class Nate and Thorn as mine as well? I knew my lady bits were voting yes for Alex and Asher, but I wasn't sure Thorn and Nate were a part of the strong protectiveness and arousal my body felt. Well, besides the connection I sensed with them from the start.

"That's not your fucking business," Nate bit out.

"It is, pup. I'm the alpha of this territory. I pick if my wolves bow to the new queen or not, and as far as I can see, she doesn't look to be fit for the role of queen."

Thorn scoffed. "Tell me you don't feel her power, Jessup Falk."

Jessup shrugged. "A mild brush of it, but is it enough for what's to come?"

What's to come?

What did he mean?

"She needs to prove herself," a woman standing at Jessup's side yelled.

"Tell me why I need to do such a thing?" I asked.

"We follow the true queen only," someone shouted.

"I don't even know if I'm the true queen or if I'm a queen at all. I've had so much shit happen tonight I can't sort them all out in such a small span of time. I just want to go in there"—I pointed to the castle—"have a goddamn cup of coffee, and work out what in the hell is going on."

This shit was starting to piss me off.

"Not before you meet our son," Jessup said.

Is my hearing going?

"I'm sorry, what?"

Some of the men around me growled low. A man from behind Jessup stepped forward. He was tall, looked like his father, but a little younger, and a scar ran down the side of his face. He smirked, and even though I was behind Nate, it felt like his eyes were drinking me in and he liked what he saw. If the licking of lips was anything to go by.

"He wants to claim the new queen as a mate. He was promised a chance to prove his strength to her. To prove he would make a good king at her side."

The air thickened around me. My pulse ate at my throat. "I'm sorry, *what*?"

"Is she simple?" someone shouted.

Jessup stepped closer. Nate tensed, and his voice came out thicker, deeper. "Do not fucking move."

It shot a ting to my clit.

Not again.

Nate's body grew in height and width, and his chest rumbled with a snarl. His tee at the back lifted a little... it had me wondering why.

"She just grew into power and arrived *tonight*, Jessup," Thorn called. "My queen won't be taking on any mate or doing anything until she can get her mind around the change in her life."

I didn't listen to their back and forth words. It seemed my nose was too interested in Nate's new scent. My hands were too interested in wanting to touch Nate. Slowly, I reached out and lifted the back of his tee.

A tail sprang free.

"Oh my God, it's so cute," I cooed and then ran my hand up and down it.

I heard Nate suck in a quick breath, and he glanced over his shoulder. His facial hair had grown, and his eyes were dark brown now instead of green, and they were wide. His mouth, which had a full set of sharp teeth, opened.

"You have a tail." I smiled, still running my hand up and down it. I heard laughter behind me. As Asher scooped me up into his arms, he ordered, "Organize this shit. I'm taking her to the castle."

"I'll bring her family," I heard Alex say before Asher had us speeding through the night toward the castle.

Yet, I wanted to go back and pet Nate some more, ideally while rubbing myself against him.

CHAPTER NINE
NATE

She'd stroked my tail.

Stroked it like it was her new plaything.

"She rubbed your tail," Jessup said, shock marring his voice.

I let out a rough sound in the back of my throat. *Tell me about it.* I could still feel her hand running up and down the length of it. My dick throbbed goddamn hard. It wanted to be buried inside of her, and now.

"Does she know what that means?" the woman beside Jessup asked.

I didn't think Paige knew anything about werewolves and how, by touching a tail in half form, it meant she'd claimed me as her own.

What the fuck had she been thinking touching me like that?

It also goddamn meant....

"Fenris, are you backing down?" Jessup asked his son.

Fuck.

If he didn't back down from his so-called claim, I would have to challenge him. I glanced over to see Alex had already ushered Paige's family away. With their human hearing, I was grateful they wouldn't overhear anymore.

Fenris threw his head back and laughed. He shook his head. "Oh, I'll be claiming the so-called queen once I've shown no one will beat me. If I have to fight *him* to prove it, to have a chance at her side, I'll do it. Then I'll override her claim on the mutt and make her bend to my will as king."

Red-hot fury pulsed through me.

"I accept the challenge then," I said loudly.

Silence drifted through the tarmac.

Fenris grinned. "Then I'll be seeing you on the next full moon, mutt."

"So be it," I snarled.

The wolves disappeared. The people were slower to move off, except Fenris who strode over to a woman, picked her up and threw her over his shoulder, slapping her ass. She squealed.

As they drifted off, leaving their alpha behind, I waited to see what Jessup had to say. His thin lips told me nothing.

"Fenris is of our blood, but he is not the right person to be in charge of command. He's been filled with visions of winning and taking his place as king, ruling over all."

Holy fuck. He was warning me if his son won, shit would hit the fan.

"It won't happen," I told them.

"I feel your alpha strength. Why have you not claimed a pack?"

I shrugged. "It doesn't interest me."

It was his woman who spoke next. "I have a feeling that's going to change."

I crossed my arms over my chest and forced the shift back to my human state while staring them down.

Their gaze swung to Thorn. "Things have been altered."

Thorn nodded. "That they have."

"Let us pray it's for the better," Jessup said.

"Who filled your son's head with such lies to begin with?" Thorn asked.

Jessup shook his head. "That I can't say. It's not pack business, but I'm sure you'll find out soon enough. Learn who to trust within the walls."

He'd said enough to let us know it was someone on the grounds. Thorn nodded once, and they both moved off, back into the woods.

Sighing, I scrubbed a hand over my face. My life had changed in a goddamn blink of an eye because of Paige Alice. I didn't have a fucking clue if it was good or bad. Though I'd argue it leaned toward bad since I had to fight for my life on the next full moon.

But shit, I knew I'd put everything I had in it because it meant it'd keep Paige out of that fucker's hands.

She'd taken me by surprise. Had cemented herself inside me even before she'd unknowingly claimed me.

In over three decades, we'd never taken time off work. Yet, there we were, willing to step back from our work as council enforcers because Paige had walked into our lives.

We'd told Thorn our purpose was to make sure Paige would stay safe. That *was* the case, but something had tugged at our chests as soon as Paige had appeared.

It pissed me off. Not only was it unexpected, but I hadn't wanted it... this connection.

However, that last part screamed bullshit, not only from my mind, but my wolf was happy with her claim over me, and that annoyed the fuck out of me as well.

"Come, let's see what mischief our queen has gotten up to." Thorn grinned.

A snort escaped. Yeah, Paige attracted trouble. She was

tough and didn't seem to care what anyone thought. No doubt she'd be up to something.

I followed Thorn into the huge-ass castle. I couldn't blame Paige for being in awe with the place. It was monstrous. On the way, I noticed Thorn receiving his own bows, but just of the head, not a full waist one like Paige had received.

Who exactly was he to them?

It was curious. Not all of them shared the same scent as Paige or Thorn. There were other species as well—humans, vampires, witches, mages, and even shifters. I'd never seen so many in one place, and all seemed to be playing nicely. It didn't happen often. Not in big groups. Actually, never in large groups; they didn't mix well. Small groups, like how I worked with Asher and Alex, yes. We were together with a common goal: to make sure everyone played well by the law.

What was the reason they mixed well together?

"For the queen," Thorn replied to my unasked question. I snapped my gaze to his. "You're easy to read. However, I'll explain more when the others are around."

Clenching my hands so I didn't wrap them around his neck and squeeze the answers out of him, I grunted. We walked across the long drawbridge and in through the gate. I caught my eyes from widening and ground my teeth together instead. I didn't want Thorn to see I was impressed. The place was like something from medieval times. Carts, straw, stalls of food, clothing, and other shit jotted around the area. It wouldn't surprise me if the shopping area led all the way around the castle.

"This is how the people make their money and pay for their residence."

"How many people live in the castle?"

"Over two hundred. The people who work the market and

the airstrip come from the village out behind the castle, and there are over one thousand people there."

Holy fuck.

"How did all this slip by the council?"

Considering the council's enforcers had never heard of this place, I could only assume it was hidden from the council. They didn't like large groups of mixed species to congregate because they were sometimes uncontrollable, and the council was all about control. Living by their rules only. If you didn't, we were sent in to deal with it.

"Our witches and mages keep us hidden. Others are repelled from the area unless they seek refuge and have sworn loyalty to the queen," he said, and added, "The old queen that was."

"It doesn't make sense. On the council there's some powerful mages and witches. They pick up on spikes of magic being used. A constant power surge would raise alarms. They would have sent a team to look into it."

Thorn smiled. "Our old queen knew that would occur. She made sure our people who designed the barrier put their work into devices she had made, which can be switched on and off only when we need to shut down the ward to allow people in. The devices are electrical and designed someplace else. The council," he sneered, the gesture prickling my skin, "doesn't detect anything from this area since the barrier also contains all magic inside."

My mind didn't want to wrap around the idea of such a place existing and how it was hiding from the council. The council had always ruled their people fairly. As far as my brothers and I knew, they were even-handed. I didn't understand why the old ghoul queen had hidden from them. We'd been following the council—their rules and all that entailed—

forever. We followed them blindly, and it was drilled into me to inform the powers that be of such a place.

Yet, I couldn't.

Thorn led us through an entryway into the stone castle. Warmth radiated throughout the place. It didn't feel over-heated, just perfect. A grand staircase stood in front of us; Thorn ascended it, and as I made my way behind him, I glanced around, catching sight of people. With a sniff, I detected a few shifters, some humans, and a couple of magic users. Some looked my way, but they all showed Thorn some type of respect with either a bow of their head or a salute. Women smiled coyly at him.

He was popular among them all. It'd make it hard if we had to take him out in the end for being a threat to Paige.

Goddamn, there I went again. Wanting to protect her.

The place was mammoth; it'd be easy to get lost. Thank fuck I had my nose. I could easily scent Paige's sweet smell down the hall we walked. She was in a room with Asher, Alex, her family, and two others I didn't know. One was a human, the other a vampire.

My ears picked up the sound of someone pacing.

Thorn opened the door in front of us. It led to a large seating area. With a quick glance, I saw the hellhound wasn't around. Paige's sister and her man didn't hold the children any longer either, and they weren't in the room, but that's all I saw before a palm connected with my face.

With a growl in the back of my throat, I grabbed the wrist and dragged her close. Paige glared up at me.

"You were out there forever. I thought they were going to have you for dinner. What took so long?"

I jerked my head back in shock. She'd been worried about me.

Me.

What the fuck for?

Asher cleared his throat, and I lifted my gaze to his, seeing his lips twitch. "We got inside and then, when I refused to allow her to go back out to, as she put it, 'kick some ass' if they tried to screw you over, she started worrying."

I opened my mouth before snapping it closed. I didn't know what to say. No one had worried about me in decades. I knew I wasn't the nicest guy to get along with, which was why I stuck to one-night stands. And I'd definitely been a dick to Paige, yet she had been concerned on my behalf.

My chest expanded. It seemed my heart liked the thought of Paige caring.

Only, my mind won out. I flicked her hand away from mine and stalked by her. "I can take care of myself," I clipped. Alex winced, and Asher shook his head. Paige's family glared at me, and Thorn snorted. I ignored them all.

A vamp and human I didn't know stood off to the side, near a tray of food and drinks.

"Asshole," I heard Paige cough out.

Ignoring it, I made my way over to the table of food, grabbed a small cut sandwich, and shoved it in my mouth. While chewing, I poured a glass of what looked like red wine.

I lifted my head to take a sip and found the vamp woman, with long red hair and cunning eyes, smiling at me. Heat hit my back. Paige's arm came around my waist and pointed at the woman.

"Don't you dare try it on him as well. You've made googly eyes at all the men in the room. *Even* my brother-in-law. I've had enough. There is no way any of them will be interested."

The woman smirked. "We'll see, won't we?"

With a snarl, Paige tried to shove me out of the way to get to the taunting bitch. Anyone could see Paige was on edge, but of course, the vamp pressed her buttons. I curled an arm around her waist, twisted and lifted her off her feet enough to walk to Alex, who sat in a chair, and deposited her in his lap.

Alex grunted, his hands landing on her waist.

Leaning in, I snapped in her face, "Calm the fuck down."

"You calm down," she spat back like a toddler.

The vamp woman giggled. Paige tried to launch herself off Alex, but his arms wrapped around her waist tightly.

"Patrice, Mesilla, out," Thorn ordered.

Straightening, I stood beside the chair and crossed my arms over my chest. The human woman scampered out quickly. Asher followed her quietly; he must need a feed.

The stupid vamp woman slowly swayed her hips across the room with a satisfied smile pasted onto her red lips. "I'll be seeing you, gentlemen." She winked. Paige sent her the middle finger before the woman closed the door.

Paige immediately settled back into Alex like it was normal for her, and Alex's face reddened. Goddamn it was funny to see him nervous. I didn't get it. Yeah, Paige was stunning, but he had to learn to control his expressions. From the look of his widening eyes, Paige had set off his cock as she shifted around on his lap. Thinking of cocks, mine perked up at the memory of Paige stroking my tail. My wolf huffed in annoyance; he wanted me to spread her legs and slip my throbbing hardness inside, claiming her right back. I clenched my jaw and threw that thought aside for now.

"Can you believe her?" Paige asked her sister.

Yasmin shook her head, her own eyes narrowed like Paige's. "She just thought all the men in the room would kiss her feet." She paused a beat. "Why didn't she care Paige is this supposed queen?" Yasmin asked.

Thorn sighed. "Vampires come here seeking peace, but they find it hard not to mix up a little drama. She will bow if it comes down to it in the end or she'll be forced out."

"Vampires are very sexual creatures," I added, noting Paige's narrowing eyes. "She was probably hoping to start an orgy."

Paige's cute nose screwed up in disgust. Her gaze moved to where Asher had been. She stood. "Where is he?" she bit out.

Ah, fuck.

If she acted how she did with the vamp woman making eyes at us, I didn't think it'd be good when she found out Asher was feeding off someone.

"He's gone to eat," Thorn said, his lips twitching.

"What?" Paige roared, then stormed from the room. Alex ran after her.

I slowly made my way to the door after Thorn. "We'll bring her back shortly... after we save the person Asher is with," I told Paige's sister and her guy. They both nodded, seeming numb from the events or possibly over the fact Paige was acting crazy possessive of all of us.

CHAPTER TEN
ASHER

If people looked closer, they would notice I wasn't myself. Pain radiated over my body from the lashings I'd received from the council. Informing them about our time off hadn't gone well. When they'd refused our request, I hadn't backed down, and they didn't like that.

It didn't matter I'd been loyal and worked decades without a break.

We were theirs to rule.

I'd had to fight my way out and had barely made it with my life. They hunted for me. I could feel them every time they'd grown close, but so far, I'd managed to escape their grasp. Since other things had happened at the airstrip, I'd yet to tell Nate and Smith, but I would have to soon.

They'd classed us as rogue.

I didn't understand why we weren't allowed our time off. Why they refused my request. Something was going on within the walls of the council. The certainty of that buzzed through me. Something rotten. Corrupt. Regardless, we would have to find out what as well as how to prevent them from searching for us.

Had I put the people here at risk? Possibly, but I couldn't see any other choice. The need inside me to get back to Paige crawled across my skin the more time I'd been away from her.

I hoped Thorn would have answers about why we had a connection with Paige Alice.

Anger washed through me once more over the council and their actions. I ground my teeth together as I second-guessed every mission we'd been sent on. Right then, I couldn't see how any of our cases had been for an ulterior motive, but I didn't know what to trust and that singed my insides.

Who had we been working for?

At least I had trust in my brothers-in-arms. I knew, since the council had acted the way they had toward me, that Nate and Alex would have my back. They wouldn't want anything to do with them until we knew for certain they weren't as corrupt as I was now thinking. We needed to eliminate the leeches from within the walls, but it would take time, and our priority right then was Paige.

So I pushed away my fury because, for now, I had to feed. The humans I'd enthralled along the way to the airport hadn't fully sated me. I needed more to bring my full strength back. I'd need it for whatever was to come.

I'd slipped out of the room earlier to follow the human down the hall. It wasn't until the end that I gained her attention by calling out, "Excuse me, miss."

She jumped and spun my way. "Y-Yes?"

"May I have a word with you for a moment?"

She glanced around, then nodded.

Smiling, I gestured her ahead of me into the room across from us. She made her way in. I followed and closed the door behind us.

When she heard the door close, her heart skipped a beat and started at a faster pace.

"Relax," I ordered. My eyes bled to glow green. She

opened her mouth, but I put my power behind the next words, "I won't hurt you. You can relax, Mesilla."

Her mouth snapped closed, her eyes glazing over, and a smile touched her lips. "Yes. Relax."

"That's right, Mesilla. I just need a nip of your blood. You'll let me, won't you?"

"Yes." She nodded and shifted her long dark hair over her shoulder.

Stepping forward, I caught her heaving chest. I could scent her arousal. Usually I would take her up on her offer, but I couldn't. She wasn't who I wanted to sink into.

Stepping close, I swept an arm around her waist, and she gasped, her eyes hooded. Leaning in, my mouth pooled with saliva at the sight of her pumping vein in her neck.

The door burst open behind us. Spinning, I snarled at being interrupted.

Paige's finger came up as she snapped, "Don't you hiss at me, Asher Evans. You." She clicked her fingers at Mesilla, who didn't move. Paige stomped across the room toward us. Alex shot through the door with Thorn and Nate following.

"Fuck, Paige," Nate clipped.

"Paige," Alex warned.

They both knew I wouldn't like being interrupted while feeding.

"My queen," Thorn called. Even he was smart enough to be cautious. They would be seeing my glowing eyes, my elongated fangs, my claws out and ready to fight for my food.

What they didn't understand was how I didn't have it in me to harm Paige.

Before Paige could reach my meal, I spun her into my arms and crowded into her space. "I need to feed," I bit out, low and harsh.

Paige's chin tipped up, her hard gaze meeting mine. There wasn't a flinch or look of worry. Instead, she demanded, "Not from her."

She didn't have a right to order me, to tell me. It infuriated me, and yet I wanted to listen to what she said. "Then who?"

"Lead her out of here, Thorn," Nate said. I tensed, ready to fight if he thought to take Paige away. I dug my claws into the rock behind Paige's head. Her sweet, intoxicating scent drilled into me. I wanted a taste, and it wasn't only her blood I wanted to have sliding into my mouth, pressing against my tongue.

Someone stepped closer. A dark growl rumbled out of me. I inched my head slightly to the side. Nate stood there. I sensed another at my other side and knew it was Smith. The hunger, my vampire side, snarled in my head to end them. But I wasn't lost yet. I knew they were brothers-in-arms.

"You never let yourself go so long without. What happened?" Smith asked.

I shuddered when tiny hands touched my stomach and slowly slid up to my chest. "Asher, you need to back off."

"You demanded me to feed on someone, Paige. Who then?"

"I-I don't know."

"Why do you think you can order us around?" I questioned, my voice as cold as steel.

"Because."

"Because isn't answer enough. Why do you get aroused? Why do you become possessive? Why do you think you own us?"

"Asher," Smith called.

Her jaw clenched. "I don't know!" she yelled in my face.

Anyone else I would have ripped their arms off for speaking to me that way.

But not Paige.

"I need to feed, Paige. I hunger, and yet you deny me what I had. Someone ready and willing. What do I do now?"

"Feed from me" came out quietly. Only it wasn't the woman I stared down at. No, she had a surprised look on her face, which I was sure matched my own. Hearing that whisper, though, had my claws and fangs retracting. My eyes dulled to my light blue color.

Slowly, I turned to face Smith. He stood, hands clasped in front of him, rocking back and forth on his feet while his cheeks shone pink.

"Smith?"

He rolled his eyes. "Alex. We're not working."

But we were supposed to have been. Working on figuring out Paige, making sure she was protected from Thorn or the people around her.

He was younger than Nate and me, by many decades, but was still valued on the team. Although, he was still very young in mind compared to us. Even in the mage world, he was a baby at thirty. A strong one, but still an infant. Hell, he had been with us for years, yet he had a lot of growing to do.

In all that time, even after battle when I needed blood, he had never offered me sustenance.

"Alex?" I questioned.

He shrugged, blew out a breath and mumbled, "Ah, Paige might be okay if you fed on one of us."

Paige's heart accelerated.

"Why not her?" Nate clipped.

"If she fed Asher, then the link between them both will be locked."

We all faced Thorn. Even as my stomach tightened in hunger, I ignored it because I wanted to hear the rest.

"Explain," Nate barked.

"Should we head back to the other room and relax there?"

"No. I want to know why my body reacts like I'm the cat and the men are catnip," Paige said. She straightened and crossed her arms over her chest. "Also, it might be good to hear it not in front of my sister and her husband. Especially Eric. He doesn't need to know my achy and needy vagina is starving for attention from three men."

The room quietened.

The heat from Alex's body hit mine. His jaw clenched. Nate fisted his hands, and I had to lock my body down. I knew all three of us were willing to satisfy her needs right in that moment. However, we had to find out why we reacted this way first.

"Speak," I snarled, my eyes locked onto Thorn's as power rushed through me.

"Things have changed. I didn't expect this to happen. But it seems when our old queen died and the power transferred to Paige, it connected us all in a way where we became her mates."

Paige made a noise in the back of her throat. "Do you mean the Australian term mates? As in friends? As in this will pass and I *haven't* dragged you all into this without any of you agreeing? Tell me I haven't fucked up your lives because my vagina suddenly sees you all as hers?" she screeched. She bent at the waist and breathed in and out quickly. I grabbed Alex by the shirt and dragged him over, pushing him toward her.

He was the best of us to console the emotional woman. I

knew I made the right choice when he started saying soothing things and rubbing her back.

Paige shook her head. "I don't even need to breathe and I'm hyperventilating." She flapped her hands up and down in front of her. "I can't breathe."

Nate snorted. "You don't need to, remember?"

She glared over at him. Her lips thinned and she stood tall, as tall as she could get, which wasn't much. "How are you all calm? I've messed up your lives. Wait." She looked at Thorn. "Have I messed everyone's lives up? Are they stuck…. Hang on. You said *all* of you. You mean you too?" Her eyes widened when he nodded. Her head jerked back, tilted to the side, and then straightened. She ran a hand through her hair. "But, I mean, I feel a connection to you. Like I had with them from the start, but I'm not a raging psycho when you're around other women."

"Just around other women or all the time?" Nate teased.

It really wasn't the time.

Her gaze, full of liquid fire, snapped to Nate. "I think I'll fire you and find another mate."

His upper lip lifted, and a growl dropped out.

"Ha!" she shouted, pointing at Nate. "Don't like the thought of that, do you?" She whipped her eyes back to Thorn. "Why don't you all go crazy with me around other men? Also, let's go back to the other thing before the douche gallery spoke. Why don't I react the same with you like I do them?"

"The link is not yet finalized until—" He cleared his throat. "—bodily fluids are shared in a sexual way. Or if Asher were to feed from you or if—"

"I got it," Paige shouted, and it was the first time a blush hit her cheeks.

Thorn nodded. "Also, once the process is completed, we will become as domineering as you are with us. Well, as you are with just them, for now."

"For now? So are you saying I'll become more attached to you as well? Jesus, am I a slut?"

Nate snorted out a laugh, Paige made a move his way, and Alex wrapped his arms around her. On contact, she seemed to calm a little. It didn't stop her death glare at him though.

"It is only humans who think more than one lover is wrong. It's accepted and mostly applied within all other races," I supplied, in hope it would ease her troubles.

I didn't think it helped. Paige's brows dipped. She bit her bottom lip and shook her head. "I-I don't think...." She took a deep breath. "I don't know what to think."

"As for myself," Thorn started, "I have noticed you didn't claim the others until they used their powers or showed their other nature. I believe that will happen once I do too."

"Then don't. I mean—"

Thorn stiffened. His amber-colored eyes flashed with a red haze over them, and he opened his mouth slightly to show us all his teeth as they grew. I caught the change that swept over Paige. Her heart raced, her eyes dulled, her lids lowered a little, and she sucked in a deep breath.

She licked her lips before one word dropped from between them in a whispered growl, "*Mine.*"

"Yes, my queen," Thorn answered, his voice deeper, harsher. "Release her."

Alex dropped his arms, and she walked her way toward Thorn slowly, a small smile splayed on her luscious lips.

The door opened, and one of the women from the plane stepped inside. Her eyes slammed into Paige approaching Thorn. She hissed as her steps ate up the carpet moving toward Paige. I started for her, as did Alex and Nate, until a huge hound bounded into the room behind the woman and tackled her to the ground.

Ezra, in his canine form, stood over the woman's back and growled viciously into her ear. It wasn't a growl of a dog, and she knew it because she froze.

Saliva dribbled out of his mouth and splattered her in the face.

Paige, in the commotion, blinked out of her haze and stared down at Ezra. Then she smacked Thorn in the stomach. But I could tell it wasn't at full-strength.

"You did that on purpose," she sulked half-heartedly. The smart-ass grinned big and wide.

Though, I couldn't say I blamed him. I would have done the same. Luckily it had already been done without our knowledge, so there wouldn't be any way Paige could shut her claim on us down.

My mind ticked it over.

She claimed us.

We were hers.

If it had been any other, I might have hated it, but it wasn't.

It was the woman who'd caught my attention so many hours ago. The woman I wanted to know. The one I'd felt a connection to even before the bond formed within her.

I knew I wasn't the only one pleased either. Alex and Nate didn't seem fazed by it. They kept an eye on her like she should be treasured as a rare prized jewel.

Even if Nate acted like an idiot, he wanted her, he liked her, and he was pleased by the events.

"Thorn, please," the woman begged.

Thorn slowly tore his gaze away from Paige and down to

her. A tick started in his jaw. We needed her gone so we could talk about the mate bond more thoroughly.

There was also the matter of my feeding.

I glanced to Alex. He sensed my stare and met it. He nodded, and I dipped my head in appreciation. Though it felt like more, like a gift. It had me looking at him differently. At the man he was becoming.

CHAPTER ELEVEN
THORN

I knew she was about to deny her claim on me; I wouldn't have it. I'd been dreaming of her for quite some time, and now that she was in front of me, I wouldn't lose her. Even after her power washed over me after mixing with mine, I worried she would be angry with what I had done. She had been a little annoyed. While I understood why, I also rejoiced in her claim, her scent, and her power surrounding me.

Like all the men in the room, others would sense the queen's claim on us.

My chest expanded from the thought of it, proud to walk about knowing she was a part of me and soon, hopefully very soon, I would have my own claim on her. I would be a part of her, and our powers together would thrive.

I didn't care she had others. It was a given she would have more than one mate, though I'd assumed it would be of our own kind. Of course, Paige was different from the late queen.

She was special.

She would bring change.

"Thorn, please," Malvina begged. Honestly, I had forgotten she'd been in the room, too captivated by Paige's beauty. I didn't want to look away, but I dragged my gaze down to the floor to see Malvina sprawled on the floor with Ezra looming over her. I thinned my lips in distaste. She'd been a thorn in my side for quite some time.

"My queen, would you call Ezra off?"

My lips twitched as I watched Paige think about it. She sighed. "Ezra, come here."

With one last growl, Ezra climbed off and strode over to Paige, who crouched and cuddled the animal close. Now *that* made my gut heat in jealousy. I wanted to be the one she cradled.

I moved my gaze back to the problem at hand. "Stand," I ordered. Malvina got to her feet. Her gaze locked onto Paige and burned in fury. She had always thought I would come back to her bed. I hadn't because six months ago, our former queen had shared what the seer had visioned for me. I would be a part of the new queen's life, and she was the same woman I'd dreamed of.

Back then, Malvina had seen my status, as the highest-ranking guard with an ear directly to the queen, as a means to gain more power over our people for herself.

I'd seen it, ended it, and she'd never gotten over it. Even though she'd been with many others since then.

"What did you interrupt us for?"

Her eyes went to the floor, and she smiled coyly. "You weren't in your room. I thought I would come find you and see if you're ready to head there."

Paige sucked in sharply, and a noise fell from between her lips. It sounded very much like a growl. I wanted to bask in her possessiveness. Some may have found her actions annoying or acted similar to how Nate had, but not I.

"Do not act like you come to my room every night. It's been *months*, Malvina, and it will never happen again."

Her upper lip rose. "Because of *her*."

"She is the new queen," I shouted. "You will bow to her."

She straightened. "I will not," she shrilled, and stormed

from the room. I went to go after her, to make her bow if I had to. She would not get away with disrespecting the queen, but then a hand wrapped around my wrist. I glanced down to see Paige had a hold of me.

Her hand fell away, and then she ranted, "I want to punch her in the tit. No, I could rip both of them off and shove them down her throat." Paige huffed. "You'll need to get your ex under control, Thorn, before I do just that."

"I was about to have words with her."

She shook her head. "Not now. We have things to talk about, and actually, no you won't talk to her. I don't like the thought of you near her." She ran a hand over her face. Her brows dipped as worry appeared over her features. "You'll need to get someone else to speak with her."

I nodded. A smile crept onto my lips. "And wipe that smile off your mouth. You got me all claimy on purpose. I've not yet forgiven you."

I bowed. "I shall seek your forgiveness in some way, my queen." I breathed out the words of the last part and glanced up at her. I caught the shiver crossing her body.

She groaned and slapped both hands to her face. I straightened, stepped close, and pulled her into my arms. Before I could say anything, she did. "I'm a horrible, terrible person."

"You are not," I told her.

She nodded into my chest. "I am."

Over her head, Asher and Nate ushered Alex forward. It seemed they didn't know what to do when our queen was upset. Alex, though, moved in close, pulling Paige's back against his chest. His hands went to her waist.

"Why do you think you're terrible, Paige?" Alex asked softly.

"How am I not? I ruined everyone's life. My sister's,

Eric's, my poor niece's and nephew's. You, Asher, and asshole." Nate's lips trembled in mirth. She shook her head again. "I'm not sure Thorn will see it as bad, but you all should. You're all here without wanting to really. I've got my stinking claim on you without knowing I did it and without getting consent in the first place." She lifted her head and moved away toward the door. "You should just leave." Her sorrow-filled gaze caught mine, and if my heart beat, it would have lurched. "If they leave, will the claim go away?"

Paige may not have noticed, but I did. Alex tensed. Nate's forehead ticked, and Asher's eyes flashed green for only a second, but I saw it. They didn't like the thought of the claim going away.

Would they show that to Paige? Make her understand they wanted to be there at her side?

"We have time to sort this out," Asher said. "For now, we should go back to your family and talk on other things, but first, I need to feed."

Paige nodded. She looked to Asher, then Alex, who was blushing, and waited.

Nate scoffed. "We'll meet you back in the room." He started for the door, grabbing Paige's upper arm.

"But... Asher might need more than just Alex," Paige said weakly. He wouldn't, the men in the room knew this. A mage's blood could sustain a vampire for longer than a human. Paige just didn't want to leave because she wanted to watch.

In a blink, Asher stood behind Alex. His mouth descended, fangs out, and latched onto Alex's neck. Alex let out a gasp and tilted his head more to the side, and then his eyes closed on a moan.

"Oh…," Paige muttered, and in the next second, the room was hit with the scent of her arousal.

My cock thickened in an instant. I held in my own groan and could tell Nate was doing the same with how hard he clenched his jaw.

Asher's eyes bled to green. He wrapped an arm around Alex's chest, bringing him back closer to his body. Alex panted out a breath. Another pulse of Paige's arousal shot into the room.

She'd be wet, so damn wet, and I wanted to slip my hand in her panties to find out.

"Fucking hell," Nate clipped. He took the couple of steps to Paige and turned her. She let out a squeal of surprise when he picked her up over his shoulder and stalked from the room with Ezra on his heel, who was making a sound which sounded a lot like a laugh.

I quickly followed, closing the door behind me.

In my years, I had been with men and women. I had a thought to stay and see if Asher's feeding led to anything more. We were all Paige's. Well, we would be, so I didn't see anything wrong in watching two of her men. We were all intoxicated on her lust. My cock throbbed, wanting release. But until I knew Paige would be for it and the other men didn't mind attention from the same sex, I would put a hold on everything.

Even if my dick hated me by the end of it.

Yet, I was sure the reward of having Paige would be worth it.

Nate shoved the door open to the sitting room we'd been in previously. Paige's sister and husband weren't around. Nate deposited Paige onto the couch and strode to the table with drinks on it. He poured himself a large glass of bourbon and sucked it down.

Paige stood, her hands on her hips. "Do you want to tell me why you took me from the room?" She glanced around, then added, "And where my family is?"

Nate growled low in his throat. He poured another drink and knocked it back. Ezra trotted over to the couch Paige had vacated and jumped up on it, lying flat with a groan. He settled in for the show.

I made my way over to Paige and curled an arm around her waist. I thought she would stiffen at my touch because it was new, but she didn't. She leaned against me.

It felt right. Perfect. My body hummed from the contact.

Too long had I been without it.

"I think, my dear, it would be best to let Nate have a moment, and I believe your sister and Eric are with the children."

She nodded, then tilted her head back to look up at me. "Why does he need a moment?"

I smiled. "We could... smell your arousal in the room, Paige. It was either remove you from what turned you on or start something you might not like."

Her cheeks heated. "Well, shit." Her tone implied she was thinking about what could have happened.

Nate picked up on it too. "Don't go down that line of thought." He drew in a deep breath, grumbled something, and poured another drink.

Yes, I could also smell a hint of what she'd felt in the other room now.

She nodded. "Right... so, ah... more talking."

My fingers traced her arm up and down. "Yes, more talking. Then I'll show you your room so you can shower before some rest."

Her brows dipped. "I slept..." She glanced out the window to the bright sun. "...yesterday. I shouldn't need to again for a while."

I shook my head. "You've changed, remember? You'll need more rest than you've had."

She shivered, and her eyes turned lazy. "I did like to sleep, so I don't mind that change."

"Good."

"Uh... if you keep going with the hand, things are about to get heated in this room," she told me on a whisper. Of course Nate heard. He shot us a glare, which Paige returned. Nate had met his match in our queen. She seemed perfect for him. For Asher. For Alex, and for myself.

Chuckling, I dropped my hands, but just for a moment. I didn't want to stop touching her. Instead, I rested them on her shoulders and massaged her. Her head dropped back, and she moaned long and loudly.

"Are you fucking kidding me?" Nate bit out when Paige's lust rose once more.

Even though I wanted to continue, I stopped my hands. Paige opened her eyes and sighed. She stepped away from me and circled her arms around her waist. Right then I wanted to punch Nate in the face.

"Maybe I need to bang you all to ease the ache. The way you all make my body crazed isn't normal. It would settle down after a quick roll in the hay, wouldn't it?" She moved to have my eyes.

"Somewhat," I told her.

"Somewhat? What do you mean somewhat?"

"From what the former queen said regarding her bonded males, the connection created is strong. The desire and possessiveness you feel will lessen after the connection is made. However, it will still be present. I'm unsure just how much."

Paige pulled a hand up to her neck. Her beautiful eyes shone with guilt.

I stepped closer to her, wanting to remind her none of us were unhappy with the bond. But she backed up, shaking her head, her eyes to the floor. "Please," she begged. "Just stay there. Whenever one of you is close, I can't think straight."

"There is something you must know then, my Paige." I waited until she looked up. "None of your men have to accept the bond. If we so choose, we can dissolve it. It will be uncomfortable for a while, but with distance, it will weaken and then drop away to nothing."

Her eyes widened. "Even though I've managed to claim you all?"

"Yes."

She nodded. "Then, that's great. All of you just have to," she seemed to choke on the next word, "leave."

"I can't speak for the others, but I'm not willing to lose you, Paige Alice."

She tensed, blinked rapidly, and then threw her hands into the air. "I don't know why you would want this. You can have a normal... well, somewhat, existence. I mean, I'm a nobody."

"You're the queen. My queen. More than that, you were made for me and I for you."

She studied me. "You really believe that?"

"With everything I am."

Her bottom lip quivered. She turned away and sniffed. With her emotions high from my confession, I wanted to continue to tell her how long I had waited for her, how much I would cherish each day I had with her. Only, as I glanced to Nate and his clenched jaw, I didn't say any more. There would be a time when we were alone, but only if she could see a future with me by her side as well.

CHAPTER TWELVE
PAIGE

His words sang inside of me. They warmed me and sent a thrill in my belly. He truly thought I was made for him and he for me.

I wanted more than anything to believe his words. But the truth was, it scared me. I'd been picked on, put down, dumped, and told I wasn't enough, and all that was from *one* man.

I had four to deal with… *if* I did in the end.

Also, I still used my human brain. Hell, less than twenty-four hours ago, I was a supernatural community of one. I didn't yet fully understand that a connection like the one Thorn spoke of was allowed. One where we were all devoted to each other. It didn't seem fair I got four men, and they only had me. Yet, the thought of any of them with someone else burned my chest.

Everything that had happened, everything I'd been through in such a short amount of time was piled too high. I worried I would tumble and break when more information got stacked on the already large amount.

A shiver raked over my skin—Asher and Alex were approaching. I spun to the door, and a few seconds later, it opened. Asher stepped in first. His previous pale complexion had a light dusting of color. He tipped his chin down at me and moved over to where Nate stood. Alex walked through next. I bit my bottom lip to stop my smile at his very heated cheeks. He closed the door, stood beside it, and put his hands behind his back, leaning against the wall.

"Everything okay?" I asked.

His eyes widened. Then he looked to the floor as he cleared his throat. "Yeah, yep. All good." He was so damn cute. Actually, cute wasn't enough since he was as hot as sin, but innocent as well, and so smart to do what he did with magic.

"Paige," Thorn called gently.

Oops. My heart had taken off in flight, and my vagina was appreciating the view of Alex a whole lot since I'd run my gaze down and he was supporting a massive erection. I had zero ideas how to rein in my reactions to them all.

Was his hard-on from me or from Asher while he drank his blood?

Oh hell... why was the thought of Alex getting turned on by Asher such a turn-on that my inner walls spasmed and my belly dipped in pleasure.

Growls sounded around the room. My body heated.

Thorn cleared his throat and clapped his hands together. "Maybe it's best we spoke of things now?"

I closed my eyes to try and clear my mind of the image of Asher and Alex in bed together. It didn't help, but I forced it to the back of my mind. I wouldn't, no, I couldn't let my body rule me. We needed to talk. We all needed answers, and then I would rest and maybe crack into pieces of guilt, horror, and sorrow.

Scrubbing a hand over my face, I nodded and headed back to the couch. "Yes, of course, we need to talk. First things first. Are you certain I'm the ghoul queen, and how did I become that way?"

Nate stayed by the table while Asher moved to sit across from me on another couch. Thorn took his place beside me, and Alex stayed by the door.

Thorn said, "Yes, I'm certain. The queen described you, and I can feel the queen's power running through you. Not only that, but your heart beats and your pupils turn a shade of red with a black ring around them. All signs the former queen had to show her power to others."

"Start from the beginning," Asher demanded.

Thorn leaned back and nodded. "Eight months ago, the queen of the ghouls announced to her bonded males and me that her seer had seen her death. She wouldn't explain how it would happen, but that it would be better for not only the ghouls but all other species. Even when we tried to gain the information to prevent her death, she refused to say. To save her people, and others, she was willing to die. The queen set out to find the one the seer saw would rule next. The one to bring us all together. You."

I sensed the color drip from my face. "How... why... I'm not...." I shook my head. "Why me?"

"You were foretold by the seer. You have a good heart, you're strong-willed, and you will fight for what you believe is right. To save us all."

"Save? What am I saving you all from?" I stood quickly, pacing the floor. "I'm twenty-five years old. A barista... and I've probably lost my job because I haven't shown up. I may have the strength of Superman, but I'm still scared of spiders. I don't understand how I'm supposed to save everyone. What happens if she got it wrong? What happens if I'm not really the one the seer saw in her vision?"

"You are," Thorn stated, his voice resolute. "I dreamed of you before the queen came to me and told me I would be a part of your uprising. Her trusted friend, who is a witch, placed a spell on me there and then. I was to be transferred to you when the time came. I left the community here to wait out until I could be by your side."

"Are you sure it was me in your dreams?" I asked, panic rising in my chest because it felt like the weight of the world was settling there.

"Yes. Completely sure."

"So what, the queen just up and changed me into a ghoul and then six months later she dies and all her powers transferred to me... how?" Too many things were running through my mind. I still couldn't believe I was the right person to be queen.

Queen.

Me.

Paige Alice.

It was fantastical to even think it. Then again, six months ago I was a human. I didn't know others existed. Now, I was thrown deep within everything.

"She disappeared the day she made you a ghoul. No one, not even her bonded mates knew where she'd gone. When she came back, she was weak. Weaker because she had made you."

"How did she make me?"

Thorn winced, and I knew I wouldn't like what he was about to say. "She cut out her own heart and replaced yours with hers."

I didn't like it.

At all.

With a shaky hand, I reached up and patted my chest. "I have her heart in me?" Thorn nodded. "Then how am I still myself and not a part of her?" It didn't feel like any of my body parts had changed. I closed my hand around my throat and squeezed to stop from gagging. I had someone else's heart inside me.

Ezra bumped his head into my side. Absently, I reached for him, and a sense of calm washed over me.

"Her heart became *yours*, Paige. You are no different."

"W-Where's mine?"

"Locked away safe."

Jesus Christ, my heart was in a jar somewhere.

"To answer your other question, the queen was betrayed by her sister Korissa. She wanted the throne, but she didn't know the queen had already chosen another to take her place. Korissa had picked the one night Marsala, the former queen, was distracted and grieving an old friend to slice her sister's head from her shoulders." I gripped my neck and looked to the floor. Thorn frowned and went on softly, "The queen's bonded mates caught her in the act. They killed Korissa... and then themselves."

My head snapped up. "What? Why?"

"They couldn't live without her and knew you would be reborn only moments after her eyes closed for the final time."

My gut twisted harshly.

They couldn't live without her.

Did that mean...? I shook my head. "We're not finishing this bond. I won't have you all tied to me to only end your lives." Ezra pushed into me more. I bit my bottom lip before it trembled. Already I didn't like the thought of them not being around if something happened to me. Already my body grew cold at the thought of anything harming them. Even if it was themselves.

Turning away, I walked to the window and looked out. I wrapped my arms around my waist. The castle bustled with people, all different kinds. I didn't know if I could be queen, but I had a feeling people were relying on me to be. For them, I would try.

However, I could put a stop to one thing. In a hard, emotionless tone, I said, "You need to leave. Asher, Nate, and Alex. Go while I've only claimed you all and the bond can still be stopped. I won't have you forced into a situation. I won't have you bound to me when... we don't know each other. You could be missing out on something else. Someone better. Thorn, I realize this is your place. I can't ask you to leave, but—"

"Don't," Thorn clipped. He came to my side and turned me with his hands on my shoulders, his grip unyielding, his eyes stony. "Do not reject us so easily."

"None of you know me. I won't fulfill the connection because you're all dropped into my mess."

"Do you not think we were chosen for you for a reason? Humans try to hunt for their one and only. They're lucky if they find that person. A lot aren't so lucky. Other races believe in finding their mate, believe in finding that one, *or more*, bonded partners for themselves. With us, we understand and accept we were born for you and you for us. It has been *seen*. It's Fate."

My eyes prickled. Tears wanted to show, but I refused them. I blinked and shook my head. "Fate can kiss my butt. I won't force anyone—"

"You won't be forcing us" came from Asher. Thorn moved aside as Asher stood. "I think we're going around in circles. We need to take this a day at a time."

"You don't have long before you have to go back for your job, right? Why not just leave now?" I suggested.

"We don't have a job to go back to," Asher announced.

The room pulsed, and then both Nate and Alex burst out with "What?"

"The council did not want us to leave. I barely made it away. It is why I had to feed again."

Nate threw out a hand. "I knew something was off. They fucking harmed you, didn't they?"

Asher nodded. "I imagine they suspect something is going on. I don't understand why they would refuse us the time off. When I told them we would be taking it no matter if they didn't give their approval, they beat me. I escaped, they hunted, I fought, and managed to flee. They'll be after us, so I'm afraid we're here for some time."

Fury bombarded my mind and clenched my stomach. My upper lip raised. "They beat you. *Hunted* you."

"Paige," Alex called.

Thorn's hand landed on my shoulders. He reassured me, "My queen, he's here. Safe."

"They beat him. Hunted him," I snarled, my gaze not believing he was whole and across the room.

Then, in a blink, Asher stood right in front of me. His hands cupped my cheeks. My skin tingled and my heart lurched. He pulled my gaze up to meet his. "I have fed. I'm whole."

"They'll pay," I told him.

He studied me, then nodded. "They will."

"You won't go back. None of you."

"We won't," Asher told me.

"But none of you can be mine," I added. I wanted them safe, even from me.

His lips twitched. "We shall see."

"Asher—"

Smiling, Asher pressed a finger against my lips and

looked to Thorn. "When we spoke of the council back at the restaurant, about how we had been told why the ghouls were extinct, you didn't like it. Do you know more?"

Asher was lucky I wanted to know the answer to this, or I would have said something more about the matter of them not being mine.

Thorn nodded stiffly. "Centuries ago, and even before my time, our kind were close to extinction, but it was due to the council members alone even before the council was created. They feared our numbers. They feared our power. Most saw ghouls as the supreme rulers and because of those things the council members conjured up stories about our kind instigating wars over nothing, of killing innocent people, and other vile things. The queen fought hard to protect her people. But with the whispered words from the wrong people, it caused the council to be formed to assist. It was then the ghouls got pushed out completely. The queen faked her own death and then took the people she had left into hiding because she knew the council wouldn't stop until every ghoul was gone from the earth.

"Over time, other species joined her, especially those with power who were deemed as a threat to the council. Before long, our group grew to a new kingdom, the size of a small town. The queen's mission was for harmony, but as always happens, corruption brewed. Hence Marsala's death by her own sister."

"The council is evil," I stated clearly after scenting Thorn had told the truth about everything. "Something needs to be done."

Asher quickly glanced to Nate and Alex. "Master Delton, and the fae king died suspiciously. Gerrid and Keilor, two of the strongest alphas are missing, presumed dead."

I tensed. I didn't like what I was hearing.

Nate's lips thinned, and worry seeped into his eyes, but he nodded. "It seems the council is culling powerful people and blaming others for it."

"We need to look into this further and expose them," Alex said. His voice was strong and held disdain. Something I hadn't yet heard from him.

What I wanted was to go to the council's door, bust it open, kick their asses and kill them for ever starting this downward spiral for my people in the first place. When I glanced to all the men, I noticed they were already watching me.

"She's angry," Alex pointed out.

Nate snorted. "What gave it away? Her fisted hands, the steam coming from her nose, or the fact her eyes are glowing?" He looked to me. "Calm down. We can't do anything about them yet."

I hated anyone telling me to calm down. I ground my teeth together.

Thorn cleared his throat, gaining everyone's attention. "It's also good that none of you are leaving since Nate has his challenge with the alpha's son during the next full moon."

Anger evaporated as I sucked in a shocked breath. "What?" I gently moved around a smiling Asher to look at Nate. I knew Thorn was changing the subject, but I allowed it and went along as I wanted to know what this was about.

Nate groaned. "Fucking great. Throw me under the bus, why don't you."

"You can't," I snapped.

Nate glared. "I can and I will."

"I won't allow it," I told him coldly. My heart already beat heavily in my chest at the thought of him fighting someone.

Nate snorted. "You don't have a say in it. This is pack business."

I bristled at his harsh words. "But you're not a part of their pack. Why are they making you fight?"

His expression shut down to a blank void. Nate shifted his gaze to beside me. "I've been up a fucking long time. I need to sleep."

"Nate," I snapped. "We haven't finished talking."

"We have." He started for the door.

"Explain to me why you have to fight," I demanded.

"Thorn, either find me a fucking room to crash in or I'll do it myself," he said, ignoring me. When Thorn glanced down at me, he shrugged and went after Nate, who was already out the door.

I didn't like to be ignored, not when he would be risking his life, and I wasn't sure why. I followed him, but Alex blocked my path.

He gave me a thin-lipped smile. "It might be best to leave him for a bit. He's never in a good mood when tired."

"Is he ever in a good mood?"

His smile widened. "Yes. Just give it time."

It seemed I had a lot of time.

A man appeared behind Alex. I quickly pulled Alex to the side and bared my teeth. He bowed low and said, "I'm sorry to interrupt, my queen. Master Thorn sent me here to show you all to your rooms."

Straightening, I cleared my throat. "Ah, right, thank you...."

The man stood tall. "Gregory, your majesty."

"Yes, Gregory." Glancing over my shoulder, I caught Alex and Asher grinning, probably over my protectiveness, which I couldn't help. Rolling my eyes, I called, "Ezra." He bounded over, panting happily.

Gregory glanced down to Ezra and stiffened.

"He won't harm you," I told him.

Gregory's lips thinned, but he nodded and moved away from the door. He started down the hall, and I followed with Asher and Alex behind me.

The walk took a million years. At least it felt like it. I listened to Gregory as he explained the rooms or areas we walked by, trying to take it all in, but I knew I would get lost all the same. I also tried to listen in on Alex as he questioned Asher quietly about the council. My gut still fired with fury.

"Wait, my sister. She's with her husband and kids. Will they be near us?"

Gregory nodded. "Yes, my queen. She has been transferred already to a room near yours and your men."

"They're not my men," I said quickly.

The guys behind me quieted, and I regretted my reply. But then, why should I? It wasn't like they were hooked on me. It was the other way around.

"My apologies. I could scent them over you. I just presumed." He cleared his throat. "It's good that they are not since, besides Master Thorn, they are not of our kind."

I stopped.

The judgmental idiot noticed and gazed at me in question.

"Take. That. Back."

His head jerked back on his shoulders. His eyes widened. "I'm sorry?"

I stepped close, felt Ezra knocking my leg, then Asher and Alex getting close. I ignored them all and told him, "Since I am the queen, I will bond, claim, and sleep with whomever I want. No one in this place has the right to judge what goes on in people's love lives unless they become a danger. Do you hear me?" I tapped his chest and then held my finger there.

I didn't expect to see a smile bloom over his face. He tipped his head down. "Of course, my queen." He turned and started walking down the hall again, continuing on with his tour.

What just happened?

Alex leaned in, his lips close to my ear, and I shivered. "I believe he's happy with your reply."

"Why?"

"He must love someone not of his own kind."

"But… that's allowed no matter their species, right?"

"Not all species would agree, Paige," Asher informed me. "Maybe the former queen was one of them."

Well, that just sucked.

CHAPTER THIRTEEN
PAIGE

Gregory opened a door at the end of yet another hallway and dipped his head. "This shall be your room, my queen. The men each have a room going down the hall from yours on each side." He turned back from my door and pointed to another door outside my room. "I believe the wolf has already taken the second door on the right. Master Thorn is in the first door on the left."

"I'll take the first on her right. Alex, you're in the second on her left," Asher said.

"I'm going in for a shower, and then I'd like to see my sister."

"Her room is at the end of the hall. A family suite," Gregory informed me.

"Thank you." I smiled, just as Ezra strolled into my room like he owned it. Gregory bowed low once more before walking back down the hall.

"Paige," Asher called. I turned just inside the room. "Do not worry about the council for now. You have a lot still to deal with here. They don't know where we are. You're safe. Your people are safe—"

"You're all safe," I interrupted, and then bit my lip for just blurting that out.

"We are. The council can wait for now. Let us worry about things in the present."

I didn't like it, but I understood why he was asking me to. There were matters here needing my attention rather than worrying about bastards who didn't know where we were. However, their time would come and soon, because I didn't like that people were living in fear outside of these walls because of the council.

"Okay," I whispered with a nod.

He smiled. "All right. Now, Alex will be taking a nap. After your shower, please don't wander the halls without someone assisting you. I'll be taking a shower too. I don't need sleep, so please knock on my door after."

I nodded. I wasn't stupid; I didn't know if my presence would be welcomed by all. Especially Thorn's conquests. My gut burned. I would take the help when offered. "Thanks, Asher." I glanced to Alex. "Have a good sleep."

He tipped his chin down and looked up at me through his lashes. "Call out to me if you need anything."

I shot him a wink before closing the door behind me. A smile crept onto my mouth as I leaned back against the door. Alex was a man I could easily fall for. Asher and Thorn were close behind him, and even though Nate drove me up the wall, I couldn't deny my attraction for him. I couldn't deny the pain I felt in my mind and stomach at the thought of something happening to him.

To any of them.

I quickly pushed that thought aside so it couldn't take hold and burn me. Instead, I glanced around the room. Though, calling it a room wasn't enough. Gregory said my sister had a family suite. This had to be one too. It was massive. A ginormous bed, bigger than any king-sized bed I'd seen, sat across the room near the windows. The gold bedspread looked soft and inviting. There were two doors on each side of the room.

One probably led to a walk-in robe, the other to the en suite. The room also contained a seating area near an unlit fireplace where a TV sat high on the wall.

"This place is bigger than my apartment," I mentioned to Ezra. He grunted at me and made his way to the bed where he jumped up and lay down, closing his eyes. Rolling mine, I told him, "I get it, you're tired." I went over to the bed and quickly kissed him on the head. "Thank you for always having my back." He lifted enough to run his wet, warm tongue over the side of my face. "Lucky I'm going for a shower." He made a noise in the back of his throat that sounded like his laugh.

Ignoring him, I made my way to the right of the room, hoping the door I approached was the bathroom. It didn't really matter since Alex cleaned me up. But I still felt the need to wash away some of the worry with the hot water.

Opening the door, shock radiated over my body. The bathroom was something out of Beyoncé's house. There was a shower that could fit easily five people in with a nozzle down each end. Not a normal two-person sink, but four. Three toilets were in small separate cubicles. There was also the biggest Jacuzzi tub I'd ever seen, a normal-sized claw-foot bathtub, and then, smack dab in the middle, were two flat, white couches. In between them was a bar.

Did they think I was going to throw a party in here?

I picked up my jaw and stepped fully in. The room was spotlessly clean, and I worried I would dirty it. Then again, bathrooms were made to be used, and there wasn't anything that would stop me from my shower.

Stripping out of my clothes, which I left on a couch, I walked to the shower and turned it on. Instant hot water soothed my shoulders; something that never happened in my old apartment. After I adjusted the temperature a little, I happened to glance back at the toilets and wondered why a castle for ghouls would need any. Only then I remembered all the other supernatural beings around the place. Of course they were needed. Then I thought why the hell was I thinking of it in the first place.

Shaking my head, I stepped under the warm spray and moaned. I tipped my head back and ran my fingers through my hair. Alex's magic was amazing, but nothing beat an actual shower after a revealing and long day.

I still couldn't believe the changes that had happened. Understanding and accepting my new life the first time after climbing out of a hole in the ground had taken me months. Yet there I was again, having to believe and trust more mind-blowing circumstances.

I was a queen.

I ruled people.

They looked up to me.

Me.

They would have expectations of my role, believing I was reborn to save their lives.

From what, I still didn't know, but if I had to guess, it would be the council. Regardless, I wasn't even sure I could be that person for them.

How the hell did someone simply become a queen overnight and be expected to rule?

I had no answers.

Had no idea how to wave that slow, weird way that queens were known to do. Did I have to talk to my people with a plum in my mouth? That wasn't me.

Yet, I found myself wanting to try.

For the ones who couldn't fight.

For the ones who need protecting.

I just wished I knew what I would be protecting them from. Again, the council popped straight into my mind. They sounded corrupted to the core.

Eventually I would find out more about them.

For now, I had things around here to sort out.

I also had four men to deal with. A vampire. A ghoul. A shifter. And a mage.

Four men who were so different to each other in their abilities and even some of their traits. Four stunningly gorgeous men who sent my mind and body into a wild spin.

Four men who I would have to keep my distance from, even when that thought felt like it cut my throat open.

For their sake, I would do it.

I had to do it.

Too much had changed in such a short amount of time, and I wasn't at the stage where any of this was normal for me in my mind.

Maybe with time…. Yeah, I wasn't even sure then.

Wanting to stay in the shower forever, I sighed, knowing I couldn't. It was tempting, though. But I wanted to see if my sister was awake. She always, okay, usually gave me good advice.

"Date them," Yasmin said as she made the bed. They'd had the chance to get some sleep, since we'd arrive late in the night, or early hours really, and I'd been busy with the men.

Maybe she hadn't heard me properly. I tried again. "Did you hear what I said? I claimed four men. *Four*. Men I don't really know, but it seemed my ghoul side wants them for herself."

Yasmin nodded. "I heard you." She faced me. "They don't seem too upset with the claim you've made. And you claiming them makes so much more sense to me now. I thought they'd put a spell on you or something, but now I know it's all coming from you it's better."

Shock swept through me. "Better?"

She shrugged. "Yes. Better because I know they're not forcing themselves on you."

"But I'm forcing myself on them."

She shook her head. "It's not the same." I glared at her. "Okay, it is. But..." She took my hands into hers. "I'm only learning about this world. You've been in it for six months, which you should have told me. They've been in this world a lot longer. I've seen you when you're all crazy protective or getting horny, freaking out about the things that have happened. They haven't. They know what they're getting into. They haven't run from your claim. They look at you like they've known you forever, like you've been theirs forever. Like you belong to them. It's not one-sided. You've claimed them, but I can tell they're happy about it and would accept and complete the bond in a second."

"They don't know me. I don't know them. This is all too much."

"I know, but you'll get used to it, and I'm here to help." She smiled. "This is our life now, and we'll get used to it together."

I sniffed. "Have I told you how you're the best sister in the world?"

Her smile warmed. "You have." She hugged me close. "Don't get me wrong, it's all scary different, but exciting at the same time." She pulled back. "And at least I'm not the queen."

I narrowed my gaze, and she laughed and went back to finishing the bed.

"Have you told the kids anything?"

"We had to because they'll see a lot of strange things around here."

I gulped. I still hated how much my sister and her family's lives had changed because of me. "What did you say?"

She glanced over at me. "Get that look off your face." She walked up to me and shook my shoulders. "For the rest of my life, I will never regret coming here with you. I was speaking with Gregory. They have a school in the town that the kids can go to. It may hold shifters and children with magic, but it's still a school, and he'd said it's an amazing one. Not only that, he told me there's a job going in town, and I thought Eric will be good at helping you organize matters around here. Things are fine. They're good even because I get to keep my kickass sister in my life. I couldn't have lived without you in it, Paige." She hooked her arm in mine and led me toward the door. "Besides, the kids are excited to see the different people. They were wondering if Tinker Bell is real."

A laugh abruptly left me.

"I know. I told them I wasn't sure, but we could find out. They dragged Eric out of here to take in some sights even before having breakfast." I tensed. "Don't worry, your ghoul guy is with them."

My body relaxed, but I quickly said, "He's not my ghoul."

"Uh-huh."

We entered the living room as their door opened, hitting the wall behind it. We both froze for a second before Nate stormed in. "Your scent lessened. Did you think for a fucking second to have woken me before you left the area?"

"I had her," Asher said, and I jumped when he stepped forward from the shadows behind us. Ezra also made it known he was there by growling low.

Nate's jaw clenched. He glanced from Asher to Ezra, then back to Asher. He ran a hand over his face. "Fuck. Fine. I'm going back to bed. You good?" he asked Asher, not me.

"Yes."

Nate grunted and then stalked from the room.

Yasmin leaned into me and whispered, "And you think they're not into you."

Nate's reaction surprised me the most. He'd scented I wasn't close even in his sleep, woke and rushed after me. Like he was ready to protect me.

I'd thought he'd hated me.

Then again, he could still. After all, he was stuck here with me, and he seemed more than annoyed, pissed even, that I'd claimed him. However, he hadn't voiced it either.

Confusion dipped my brows.

I glanced to Asher. He was already watching me. Earlier, when I'd gone to his room knocking and asked if he wanted to come with me to see Yasmin, he had, without questioning it. He followed me down the hall, a couple of steps behind. I'd felt his eyes on me the whole way, and I'd enjoyed the lick of heat they produced over my body. I may have even put an extra swing to my hips.

I did like their attention.

I liked them.

"Tinker Bell doesn't exist. Fairies do though, but keep the children away from them because they're vicious creatures."

Yasmin's mouth gaped. My throat thickened. Did that

mean he'd heard everything we'd talked about? Stupid, stupid me had thought a room separating us would be enough. I should have realized it wouldn't. Although, I had slightly forgotten he was around because talking with my sister consumed my mind.

Asher stepped closer to me. "Your sister is correct. We know what we're getting into."

My body stilled. I opened my mouth to say something but squeaked when he flashed forward so fast it was hard to track. He stopped right in front of me. Yasmin let out a gasp and took a step back.

Asher leaned in. "I cannot speak for the others, but I enjoy the idea of being yours. Of having your claim upon me." Slowly, he reached up and tucked a strand of hair behind my ear. "I understand everything that has happened is unnatural for you. I'm hoping with time you will finalize the claim. Until then, know I'll be waiting, at the pace you set."

My heart jackrabbited in my chest. He glanced down, as if he could see my heart under the shirt I'd found on the bed when I'd finished my shower. His lips lifted in a smirk.

The room suddenly felt a lot smaller when he pulled his eyes up, and they were heated with desire.

"Oh my," Yasmin whispered.

"Mommy" was called by a six-year-old monster as Sophie ran into the room.

Asher stepped back, moving his gaze from mine to the doorway, but I couldn't drag my eyes from the man in front of me.

He wanted me.

He liked that I'd claimed him.

He was willing to take things at my pace.

What did I do with that information?

"Hello," I heard Sophie say. "I'm Sophie. Who are you?"

"Asher Evans."

"You're very pretty," Sophie commented, and that seemed to snap me out of my state since I stepped in front of Asher and faced Sophie.

Yasmin, who was beside her daughter, gave me a look. I shrugged. I couldn't help my reactions. They were irrational when it came to the four men.

Asher's chuckle swept over my head. Glad to see he found it funny how I was protecting him from a six-year-old's gaze. His hands landed on my shoulders, and I melted into his touch.

"Are you Auntie's boyfriend?" she asked as Ezra made it to her side and licked her face. She giggled and wrapped her arms around his neck. Yasmin just watched on. She seemed okay now with the thought of Ezra near her daughter.

"Who's Auntie's boyfriend?" Oscar asked as he stepped through the door with Eric and Thorn following. Oscar's eyes narrowed on Asher behind me. "Who're you?"

"Oscar, this is Asher. A friend of your Aunt Paige's," Yasmin explained.

Oscar studied Asher for a moment. "Are you different too?"

"Yes," Asher stated simply.

"Are you like Mr. Thorn and Aunt Paige?"

"No. I'm a vampire."

I balked at the honesty. Yasmin and Eric didn't seem fazed by it at all; they both looked to their son for his reaction.

Oscar's eyes widened. "Cool."

"Mommy, we saw so many things out there. One boy even changed into a big pussy cat right in front of us. It was awesome," Sophie exclaimed with a cry of joy.

"That's..." She glanced at Eric. "...great?"

Thorn smiled. "I think the young boy was taken with Sophie and wanted to show off."

Yasmin's lips thinned. She clearly wasn't sure how to react.

"It was harmless, babe," Eric reassured her.

"So you drink blood," Oscar said, coming close our way.

The mention of blood had me thinking of Asher drinking from Alex. I tightened my legs together when my walls convulsed.

"Oh, look at your eyes," Sophie cried, and all of a sudden, I wanted to throw a bag over Asher's head and drag him from the room.

This was getting ridiculous.

Grinding my teeth together, I locked my emotions down and glanced over my shoulder to witness Asher's eyes bleeding back to his normal color. A groan slipped past my lips as his hands drifted down to my waist and gripped.

Would it be wrong to rub my butt on his crotch?

"Why do they change like that?" Oscar asked, and it was like a cold bucket of water being thrown over my lust.

There're kids present, Paige. Get your head out of the gutter.

It was all Asher's fault for practically telling me he wanted me and then touching me and showing his eyes off. Damn him.

"He was just showing you something he could do," Thorn said quickly.

"What else can you do?" asked Oscar.

With a breeze lifting my hair, Asher was no longer behind me, but standing on the other side of the room. Sophie laughed and clapped. Oscar's mouth dropped open.

Asher's smile caused my belly to roll in pleasure.

"This place is amazing!" Sophie yelled.

"It's pretty cool," Oscar said. He tried to wipe the big smile off his face to act the cool kid but failed. "Can you go out into the sunlight?"

"Yes." Asher smiled.

"Can you eat normal food as well?" Oscar questioned.

"Yes, and drink other things besides blood."

"Does your skin sparkle when you go outside?" We all turned to Yasmin who'd been the one to ask that question.

Asher chuckled. I looked back to watch, the sound making my heart happy.

"I think that's enough questions for now. How about the two youngest in the room go wash your hands before the food Thorn arranged arrives?" Eric said. Both kids ran off, heading toward the bathroom off their room. The place was amazing. Yasmin had shown me through before, and the suite was more like the size of a home.

Oscar paused at the doorway. "Will you still be here when we come out?" he asked Asher. I didn't even get a look in.

Asher glanced to me, and I couldn't think of anything else better than spending time with my family and him. I nodded.

"I'll be here," Asher replied. Oscar's grin widened before he nodded and disappeared to wash up.

CHAPTER FOURTEEN
ALEX

The room they supplied was extravagant. It was like a mini penthouse suite. All I wanted to do was rest. Except I had to do something first.

My dick had never been so hard for so long. Between my reaction to Paige and Asher feeding on me, I was already close to coming in my pants. All worries about the council, what my family would think, and the new life I'd been thrust into was at the back of my mind. At the forefront was the feel of Asher's teeth sinking into me, the way desire shot straight to my already hard cock. Already so damn hard because of the woman who had claimed me.

Me.

Alex Smith.

Top of his class mage, but a fuckup still in my parents' eyes because I hadn't married Emily Fortier to secure their ranking in the mage world.

Paige Alice wanted me, not because of status, but because I was meant to be hers.

She was meant to be mine, and I wasn't scared about it like I had been with Emily. This felt right.

But what would have happened if someone else had been on the team or it was another team altogether in the restaurant when Paige's powers rose? Would the result still be the same?

Would she have claimed another or waited until our lives collided?

I didn't know, but time would tell when another used their magic or power in front of her. I'd see if she'd claim them. If it was only because of the power....

My dick shrank at the thought of it.

I'd always been a worrier. Overthought things. It was exactly what I was doing now. Should I just accept that fate had intervened, and I was meant to be claimed by Paige?

Time would tell, I supposed.

There was no denying the attraction I felt for her, though. She was beautiful, even in her smaller package. Saying that, her temper made up for her tiny size. While we barely knew each other, without a doubt she was perfect for me, and I couldn't wait to discover more about her.

God, I could still sense her arousal when Asher had bitten me. My dick, once again, hardened. Not only from thinking about Paige, but from the bite itself. I didn't know a vampire's bite would feel like that.

I would have come in my pants if Asher had fed while Paige watched or touched herself.

Walking into the bathroom, I palmed my rigid cock. I turned on the shower and stripped from my clothes, wondering why I wasn't fazed by offering Asher my blood. Drinking from the neck seemed intimate, almost personal. The knowledge threw me for a loop.

I was attracted to both men and women.

Asher and Nate, and even Thorn, were all good-looking guys. There, I'd finally admitted to myself I could appreciate their looks without anyone knowing.

Under the spray of water, I took my cock in hand and stroked slowly. I moaned, closing my eyes.

Would Paige have found it erotic if I pushed myself back on Asher? I'd felt his erection just touching my ass. Thinking about it then, I moved my hand over myself faster. Would Paige have liked to have seen Asher reach around and palm my dick? From the look in her eyes as he'd drank, it seemed like she would have enjoyed it. If not, she wouldn't have gotten turned on watching Asher clamp down on my neck.

"Goddamn," I grunted.

I wished I'd had the courage to have taken the moment further between us all. Even with Thorn in the room. He'd also seemed to look on with desire in his eyes.

As I stroked over my length, I pictured Paige and Thorn approaching. Asher already had his hand over my pants while he rubbed himself into my jean-clad ass. I thought of Paige dropping to her knees, undoing my pants and pulling me free while Thorn got to his knees and cupped Paige's breasts. Nate stood to the side with hooded eyes watching us all while he pleasured himself, then Paige would lick the tip of my dick, drawing a groan from my mouth like I was right then in the shower.

Thinking of Paige taking me into her mouth was enough for streams of cum to shoot out the tip as I moaned long and deep.

Never had I been so damn turned on before. If a simple fantasy drew such a reaction from me, I couldn't wait to see where this bond between us all would go.

The bathroom door suddenly opened, hitting the wall with the force behind the shove. Nate strode in wearing jeans only. Alertness rocked through me. I shut off the shower and climbed out, grabbing a towel and wrapping it around my waist.

"You gotta help me," he growled.

"What's wrong? Is it Paige? Is she all right?"

"No," he clipped, and then stormed back into the large space that doubled as a living room and bedroom. I grabbed another towel to dry the rest of me and followed.

"What's going on?" I asked, watching Nate pace at the end of the bed.

"I can't stop fucking thinking. Put a spell on me or do something to knock me out for a few hours sleep." He ran a hand roughly through his hair. "I keep thinking she won't be safe unless she's next to me. There ain't no way I'll ask her to go to sleep so I can get some shut-eye." He flung the blankets back on my bed and took off his jeans. I saw a flash of skin before he got in and covered himself. With my blanket.

I choked. "What are you doing?"

"I need to sleep. If you knock me out and if I feel someone's sleeping next to me, then I might actually get some rest."

He was seriously on edge. If he didn't get sleep, there was a chance Paige and Nate would butt heads. But… he was in my bed, and he wanted *me* to sleep beside him.

There was also the fact he was naked.

Naked.

"First of all, get on some damn pants."

He rolled his eyes, like being naked around me meant nothing to him. Then again, shifters never gave a second thought about being in the nude. "Smith, just get in the fucking bed. Knock me out."

Glaring, I conjured up two pairs of boxers and threw a pair at the cranky wolf. He grumbled but slipped them under the blanket and put them on. I pulled mine on and up under the towel, then dropped the towel to the floor. I made my way to the bed and moved the blanket up to climb in, only to pause. Even though I'd just come, the sight of Nate's erection caused my dick to jerk. I clenched my teeth and groaned inwardly.

I was getting turned on by everything and everyone.

"What?" Nate snapped. He glanced down. "Yeah, it won't go down."

"Didn't you…?" My face heated. There wasn't a chance in hell I would finish that sentence.

"Yes. Goddamn twice."

I sighed and dropped the blanket before scrubbing a hand over my face. This was so damn awkward. We'd been teammates for five years and never had we talked about our dicks before. We worked, we got along, and we were like brothers to a point, but never had I thought, besides them being good-looking, about the what-ifs between us.

As far as I knew, neither of them swung that way.

I shouldn't have been thinking about that shit then either. Nate was there for my help. Sighing again, I took the blanket, slipped in, and rolled so Nate had my back.

"You gonna knock me out?"

"What happens if I do and you don't wake up from it? I don't have a bloody timer on my spell. Depends on the person. You could be asleep for half an hour or ten hours."

He cursed low, probably thinking about the times I had used my knock-out spell in combat. Those times were always to complete a quick mission and to get in and out. We never lingered, so I didn't have a clue how long it lasted. Maybe I should have tested it on someone.

"Want me to test it on you?" I offered.

He growled in the back of his throat. "No."

"Then you'll just have to go to sleep next to me." I closed my eyes and took a deep breath, trying to relax. But knowing the man, a guy I'd worked with for a damn long time, was awake behind me probably staring at the roof.... Nope, he shifted. I felt him sit up, slap the pillow, and fall back onto the bed. His legs moved restlessly. Up, down, up, down, over and back, I was ready to chop them off.

Rolling, I shifted close, put my leg over his, my arm over his chest where I grabbed his arm and tucked it close to his body while I rested my head near his shoulder. His body locked tight, but I ignored it, intent on getting some sleep.

"Sleep," I ordered.

"What the fuck are you doing?"

"If you move around the whole time you're in here, I won't get any sleep."

He didn't move, but he was still stiff in my arms. His breath skimmed my face; it smelled like bourbon.

A snort dropped from Nate's nose. "Never thought this'd happen."

I chuckled. "What? Us in bed or having Paige claiming us or being rogue from the council?"

"Fuck. All of it," Nate muttered, his body finally relaxing.

"I'd defy the council any day if in the end it means Paige is in my life," I told him. Without her, I doubted my life would have changed. I would have lived the days doing the same thing over and over. Following the council's missions. Working with men, but not really knowing them.

I never would have been charmed by Paige, opened my eyes to change, and offered my blood to Asher or my comfort to Nate. Not until she'd come crashing into our lives.

She was altering our world for the better, and it had started right away, even back at the restaurant. When she'd walked through my ward. Her being new to the world, to the differences our world presented, meant taking things slow. She was freaked over claiming us unknowingly and didn't understand how women of her status would and should have more life mates than one.

"She's gonna be a pain in the ass," Nate grumbled, his voice lower.

I couldn't help but laugh. "And you'll like it." I knew he would because he enjoyed going head-to-head too much with her. Not many would argue against Nate. Paige did, and he enjoyed it.

He scoffed. "Nah."

"Uh-huh."

He quieted, and just when I thought he'd drifted off, he whispered into the room, "Why isn't this weirder?"

It was my turn to tense. I opened my eyes and stared at his skin in front of me through hooded eyes. I knew what he meant—us lying next to each other. Hell, I was practically on top of him, and yet I didn't mind it.

"Maybe it's got something to do with Paige, the connection we had with her even before her claim."

"Hmm, maybe," he mumbled, and then in the next second, his breath evened out and his whole body sank deeper into the mattress. He was asleep.

I should have rolled away, but I didn't. Instead, I lifted my head slightly and glanced at Nate. In his slumber, he looked younger. There wasn't a permanent scowl on his face, though, which surprised me. I'd thought it'd still be there.

Then it felt strange I was staring at him.

Thinning my lips, I rolled over, giving him my back. Shock rippled through me and my stomach twisted in a good way when Nate moved with me. With an arm over my side and curling across my stomach, he pulled me back into the curve of his body.

My dick decided it was time to party and jerked behind my boxers.

I squeezed my eyes closed and thought of my family, which helped the erection to deflate, and finally, I got some sleep. The warmth from Nate's body lulled me into comfort.

CHAPTER FIFTEEN
ASHER

"Maybe we should let them sleep longer?" I suggested. At first I had been shocked to see Nate and Alex in bed together, but I had a feeling Nate would have been on edge and needed some type of comfort to get to sleep so he didn't worry about Paige. Not that she would know it or he would admit to it. On the surface, Nate was hard, but deep down, very deep, he was soft. He cared, and Paige had touched that caring side to him.

"Do you have a phone on you?" Paige asked with a wicked glint to her eyes.

My lips twitched. "Unfortunately I don't."

"Ezra, run and steal Yasmin's phone," Paige said, and Ezra bounded from the room. She nudged her hip with mine. "If I didn't have the meeting Thorn organized with the queen's advisers, I would let them sleep, but I have a feeling they'll want to be present."

She was right. Plus, they'd gotten enough sleep. Six hours had gone by that we'd spent with Paige and her family. The children were a treat to be around while they learned new things.

"You're correct," I answered.

I didn't trust anyone here with Paige besides her family, my men, and Thorn. She needed all the protection she could have when meeting with others who had been sworn to the former queen.

I heard Ezra approach before he ran into the room. I still found it unbelievable a hellhound, a creature from Hell itself, was linked to Paige. Not only that, but he acted like a tamed domestic dog. He was smarter than others we'd fought. He kept his power locked tight, which was how we hadn't sensed what he was to begin with. It made me wonder if he was superior to all other hellhounds. But also, how did he find his way to be with Paige? Something I would ask and soon.

When Paige held out her hand, Ezra dropped the slobbery phone into it. Paige wiped it on her pants, like it was nothing to her, then held it up in front of her. She giggled as she snapped a couple of pictures before moving to the side of the bed and taking some more.

Nate's eyes snapped open, landing on Paige. She waved the phone at him and grinned like a maniac. Nate growled in the back of his throat, causing Alex to open his eyes. He froze at the sight of Paige who stood in front of me. I saw him move slightly and then his eyes widened when he realized Nate was still behind him.

"Paige, give me the fucking phone," Nate clipped.

"Nope." She grinned. "It's too cute to delete." She let out a squeal and bolted behind me when Nate jumped from the bed for her.

"Asher, move," he demanded.

I smirked, crossing my arms over my chest and cocking an eyebrow.

Nate cursed. "Paige, I swear to fucking Christ, if you don't get rid of those photos, I'll… do something."

Paige laughed. "Sure, okay. I'll get rid of them."

We all heard the lie in her voice, could taste it in fact.

To try and control the situation, I shifted the conversation to why we were in the room in the first place. "We wouldn't have woken either of you, but there's a meeting in half an hour with the advisers of the former queen. Paige wanted us all there."

Nate straightened before nodding. "I'll get dressed," he bit out and then walked out of the room, slamming the door behind him.

Glancing back to Alex, I should have expected it, but his cheeks were burning. I could still taste his blood in my mouth. It had been intoxicating. Rich and filled with power. I wouldn't have to feed for a long time. However, I wanted another nip. I also wouldn't mind scenting his arousal and Paige's mixed together as it had been in the room earlier.

I had never thought of Alex any way besides working alongside him.

Until I'd tasted him.

Until I knew he'd been aroused by my bite.

Usually men enjoyed it, but not to the point of getting hard from it like Alex had. Unless they were interested in men. Did that mean Alex was?

I had been around so many years and enjoyed both men and women. I also liked the thought of young Alex being turned on by my bite.

Right then, his gaze swiftly raced over me and then Paige before moving to the floor. I smiled when his blush raced down his neck. What had he been thinking to cause such a delicious reaction?

He cleared his throat and sat up, pulling the blanket with him to cover his waist.

Christ, was he hard now?

"So, ah, I'll get dressed too," he said, then waited.

"Go on then," Paige teased; she was reading him along with me. She knew he was embarrassed and turned on. I drew in his scent, and the peppery aroma to his lust thickened.

Alex coughed. "Right." He nodded. "Um, if you'll just give me a moment."

Ezra let out a noise that sounded like a laugh. I glanced to him as he looked up, and the damn hellhound rolled his amused eyes before walking to Paige and nudging her legs.

Paige laughed. "All right, I've had my fun." She winked at Alex. "See you soon." She walked from the room with Ezra and then called back, "I'll be in my room. Meet me there."

Once she was gone, I turned back to Alex. He paled. "Nothing happened. We just slept beside each other. It might have looked different with Nate close, but it wasn't. He couldn't sleep because he was thinking about Paige. He was worried and wanted to go to her side, but he needed sleep so he wouldn't be so cranky. I'm not sure if it helped since Paige has taken photos."

My lips twitched. I didn't understand why he was trying to explain himself to me. Still, I found it amusing.

"I'm sure it won't happen again and, ah, the team will be as it always was…."

Ah, now it all made sense. He was concerned I would think the group dynamics would be harmed. I shook my head. "Alex, nothing has changed between the team. I'm not worried if things change between the team either. I understand what happened here, and you shouldn't feel you have to explain yourself to me. I'm not in charge any longer. We work together as one. After all, I'm sure we all want to make sure our mate is safe."

His eyes widened. "You've accepted this?"

I nodded. "I'm not a fool to fight it when I can feel the pull toward her. Paige is mine. Yours. All of ours. I've informed her I'm not going anywhere. I would like to finalize the bond, at her own pace."

"Should I tell her that as well?" he blurted. His action and words were endearing, and oh so sweet and innocent.

"That is up to you."

"I do want this bond."

Another smile graced my lips. I hadn't smiled so much in a long time. "I know."

"And you're good with sharing her?"

I would share Paige. I also hoped I would share something more than just a collaboration with the men. Only time would tell if that would happen. Maybe the bond with Paige wasn't the only one. I'd felt a connection toward Nate and Alex since I'd met them more than any others I'd worked with, which was why I'd chosen them to work on my team. I even felt one with Thorn, despite him pissing me off the first time he appeared. Though, I'd ignored it until we'd arrived here.

"I am."

He nodded, seeming lost in thought. Then he said, "So am I."

"I can see Nate agreeing eventually," I mentioned. "Thorn, of course, is all in."

Alex snorted. "Thorn is a given, and Nate's just being stubborn, but she'll wear him down."

I smiled. "I agree." I glanced over my shoulder, feeling the need to get back to Paige.

"Go, I'll be there in a second. In fact—" He clicked his fingers and was dressed in jeans and a shirt. "I'm ready now." He got out of bed.

Turning, I walked to the door, down to Paige's room, and entered without knocking, knowing Alex would follow because the destination was our queen.

We found her sitting on a chair, her gaze already on us. Her smile was radiant. If my heart beat, it would have stopped because I couldn't describe how beautiful her smile was. She pointed at the fire, which Ezra lay in front of, as if we didn't see it. "Look, they lit it."

I returned her smile because hers was contagious. "I can see."

She rested back in her chair. "Do we have to meet those advisers yet?"

"You are queen. I'm sure Thorn would push back a meeting for you," I told her, but then added, "Although, it is probably best to get this out of the way."

She groaned, and my cock jerked, my mind going to the sounds she would make once I was inside her. When I caught Alex adjusting himself, I knew he clearly had the same thought.

She nodded and stood. "You're right. Let's get this out of the way." Ezra grumbled as he climbed to his feet and accompanied Paige as she made her way toward us. Passing by, she ran a hand over my arm, then Alex's before walking out the door. We followed. We would always follow Paige. Even not knowing her for long, our connection was strong. And I already knew I never wanted a day without her in it.

As we went by Nate's door, it opened with a bang. He strode out with a scowl and stepped in beside Paige. She smiled up at him, and when his eyes narrowed down on her even more, she giggled.

"I will get those pictures."

She reached out and patted his arm. "Uh-huh."

Nate growled under his breath but said no more because Thorn appeared at the end of the hall. Paige's smile widened and she waved. Thorn returned the grin and waited for us.

"My queen," Thorn said with a smirk and a bow when Paige glowered at him. "Right this way." He turned and headed down another hall. We walked on silently. Thorn had informed Paige and me, which I would tell Alex and Nate, that our private rooms were soundproof. The rest weren't, so we would have to watch what we said.

As we moved further into the heart of the castle, the hall became busier with people. I could sense my own kind among them, as well as others. They all looked, and most bowed to Paige. It was the ones who didn't I took extra care to study— memorizing their faces and their scent.

Ezra pulled back his upper lip and snarled at a man who got too close to Paige. I stepped forward to get between our queen and him, but he simply dropped to his knees and pressed his forehead to the floor. "My queen." He breathed the words.

Paige's eyes widened. She glanced to me, Thorn, and then to the man on the floor. I heard a muttered, "She's out of her element. Some queen she'll be."

Paige tensed. She clenched her jaw and straightened before saying, "Rise, sir."

The man sprang up like a jack-in-the-box. His eyes never made it to Paige's, though; they stayed on the floor.

"Are you after something?" Paige asked.

"If you would be so kind as to allow my mate to see the doctor, she is close to giving birth, and I worry if she does it alone, there will be problems."

Paige's head tilted to the side. "What do you mean allow her to see a doctor? Can't she already?"

Someone scoffed. "Not when the doctor is ours." A witch stepped forward.

"Address the queen properly, Rylee," Thorn demanded.

When Rylee rolled her eyes, Nate's chest rumbled with a growl. The witch bowed her head half an inch and said, "My queen, we do not let our doctor work on animals."

Paige's hands fisted and she faced the woman completely. "Are you saying because his mate is a shifter, the witch won't help her through her birth?"

"Yes."

A door at the end of the hall opened and an old mage came through. "Queen, that is the way it has been for so long. They will have to seek the doctor from the wolf pack. We do not help them."

My upper lip rose. I wanted to rip the arrogant smirk off his face.

Anger burned bright in Paige's eyes. "Who are you?" she demanded. My lips dropped, and I fought a smile. She'd been worried about being queen, and yet even from the first moment I'd seen her to right then, I felt there was something important about her, and now I could tell she would be fine in her new role.

"Odin Servetus. The magic users' chairman and trusted adviser to the former queen."

The man beside Paige dropped to his knees. "The wolves won't help when we're not a part of the pack since we're horse shifters."

Paige's hand landed on the man's shoulder. He stiffened. "What's your name?"

"Michael Dill, my queen."

"I will find someone to help your mate, Michael."

Michael made a noise in the back of his throat. It sounded like a sob. "Thank you, my queen. Thank you. Thank you."

"It won't happen, you cannot—"

Paige's gaze snapped up at Odin. "Are you telling me

what I can and can't do?" Her voice was hard and cold. My cock jerked once more.

Odin blanched and replied gently, "Of course not, my queen. I only advise."

People murmured around us. Paige ignored them all and said to Michael once more, "After we speak in here, I'll have Thorn come to you and let you know who will attend your mate."

Michael nodded, his hands clasped in front of him as if praying as he thanked her over and over.

Paige patted his shoulder once more and then strode forward. Ezra and Nate kept at her sides, while Thorn and I moved to her back with Alex behind us.

Odin moved aside, bowing his head as Paige walked by. As soon as all of us had entered the meeting room, the door closed. Paige made her way to the seat at the end of the table. Once there, she stopped at the side of the chair and eyed the six others in the room—three women and three men, including Odin.

Thorn pulled out her chair and she sat. Pride filled me. I knew she'd be nervous, but she hid it well and looked regal. Nate stepped back to lean against the wall behind her with Alex. They both had their jobs and knew, without my telling them, to keep an eye on all the people in the room. I moved to them as well, but my objective was Paige. I would keep an eye on her emotions and guard her with my life, like Thorn and Ezra were. Ezra planted himself on Paige's right. Her hand landed on his head and she gently rubbed over his fur. Thorn stood tall on her left.

"Shall we get started," she called clearly.

CHAPTER SIXTEEN
PAIGE

Fury still consumed me.

I wanted to shout and yell at everyone. Instead, I controlled it, even though it was hard. I needed to get to the bottom of the issue to fix it, because I *would* have a doctor or even a nurse visit Michael's mate by the end of the day.

Odin stood at the other end of the table, while the others took their seats slowly. Odin cleared his throat. "Queen Paige Alice, I have already introduced myself, but let me introduce you to everyone else." I nodded. He pointed to his right where a man, who looked Odin's age, in his forties if I had to guess, sat. Though, I knew they could be older than what they seemed. Even thousands of years old. "This is Barrett Caldas, mage."

Barrett didn't bow. He stared me down, causing Ezra to growl. It seemed, also like Odin, he was a cocky bastard. Next to him sat another man, but he appeared younger, not by much though. I hated how looks were deceiving.

"Beside him is Clyde Rick, head vampire." Clyde dipped his chin at me, but his eyes were to Asher behind me. I didn't like it. Odin pointed a hand to the left where three women sat. The first looked to be in her late sixties, the next in her forties, and the last seemed sixteen. Shock slid through me. Odin gestured to the first. "Alma Burnet, seer." Alma didn't bow or dip her head. No, she winked at me instead. I smiled in return. My shock over her age subsided slightly, but I still wondered if seers aged differently to witches and mages, who all seemed stuck in their forties, or did it mean Alma was as old as time? Odin shook his head and sighed. "Grace Hatty, witch." Grace stared at me coolly and then reluctantly dipped her chin down about an inch. "Lastly, Selma Bobbie, vampire." Selma glanced away from behind me at my men, causing my irritation to flare. Then she smiled sweetly and bowed her head while Odin took his seat at the end of the table. I didn't trust her, and it wasn't only because she'd been eyeing my men. There was an untrusting glint in her gaze.

Still, should I class them as my men?

Yes, I could, and I would. They were mine until they got smart and ran for the hills so I could protect them from this new change.

Until then, I would make sure people knew they belonged to me. Without a doubt, I was about to become a possessive bitch. Leaning forward, I rested my elbows to the table and clasped my hands in front of me. "It's a pleasure to meet you all," I said. Then I gestured to Thorn with a flick of my hand. "All of you would already know Thorn. At my back is Alex, Nate, and Asher. Also, beside me is Ezra." I patted his head. He leaned into it and panted. If Asher and the others didn't know Ezra was a hellhound until he changed, then these people wouldn't either, and I wasn't about to tell them. Not when they screwed their noses up at me when I'd introduced him. They thought he was beneath them all. He wasn't. They'd find it out eventually.

"I didn't realize Thorn would be... so close to you already," Odin commented. "He was, after all, just the former queen's high-ranking guard."

The shmuck looked down on my Thorn. What was strange was how I'd already thought they knew Thorn and the men were my bonded mates. I chanced a brief glance at Alma. Had she been the seer to inform the queen of everything? Alma's wicked smile and wink my way told enough. They had kept it between her and the queen, maybe even her mates and Thorn.

Reaching up, I took Thorn's hand in mine and brought it around to my lips where I kissed it. Looking up at him, I found him already gazing warmly down at me. A smirk played on his lips. I heard a cackle and knew it was coming from Alma. I had a feeling I would like the woman a lot.

Glancing back to Odin, I asked, "Did you know I would be showing so soon?"

Odin flicked a glance to Barrett and then Thorn. His jaw clenched. "No. As far as we knew, Thorn was on a mission to see what the council were up to these days. We were aware a new queen would arise, but when, we didn't know. Still, we were preparing for it." He glared down at Alma, who ignored him completely and kept smiling at me.

"Funny how the former queen's trusted advisers weren't informed," I mentioned.

"Are you saying Thorn is your mate?" Grace asked.

"Yes. Along with Alex, Nate, and Asher."

A fist pounded into the table. All eyes shot to Barrett. "This is an outrage," he bellowed. "They're different species. You can't have them as your mates."

Ezra got to his feet and snarled.

The room thickened with my rage. I sensed Alex, Asher, and Nate step closer to my back. I dropped Thorn's hand and stood, leaning into my hands on the table. "Are you telling me who I should have as mates?"

Odin stood too, his hands pressed down on the air in front

of him. "No. He was just surprised, as we all are. He means no harm by it."

That I doubted.

"Ezra, go and get Eric for me. Only Eric," I told him without looking away from the people in front of me. Ezra huffed and went to the door with Nate following. He opened it for Ezra to slip out. Nate stayed standing by the door with his arms crossed over his chest, scowling around the room.

"Since I'm new here, I'd like to get some things that are concerning me out of the way. From what I've seen and heard, can someone tell me, even though we have mixed species within our community, it's still segregated?"

"Of course," Barrett snapped.

"Did the former queen allow mixed races to bond?"

Barrett's face scrunched up, even Grace and Odin looked disgusted by my question, but it was Clyde who answered with, "We've been around for many, many years, my queen. It is frowned upon being with someone from another race. The former queen was advised to keep peace in the community, it would be better to segregate the races."

"It is treason to be with another kind than your own," Barrett yelled.

Clyde turned to him slowly. "And yet, the former queen never once killed or sent away anyone when she found out what was happening behind closed doors."

"Because it never happened under her ruling."

Clyde laughed. "You are a fool to think it didn't. It happened, and Marsala knew of them all. She made sure to know of it to protect them from the likes of you and the people who follow your lead."

Barrett stood, his chair flying back. "How do you know this?"

Clyde smiled, flashing a bit of fang. "Because I was tasked to find out about them all and inform her." While Barrett shot daggers out of his eyes and breathed deeply, Clyde looked back to me. "She knew it wouldn't be for her to change things. It would be for the next queen to do so because you have already changed many things by taking a vampire, a shifter, a ghoul, and a mage as your mates."

All right, Clyde wasn't too bad of a guy. Especially if he went behind Barrett, Odin, and Grace's back about different species getting together. Selma I didn't trust as yet, since she sat quietly with a flirty smile on her face staring at Asher. Of course, it was my right to step in front of him more to block her view. She smiled when I glared down at her.

Clyde brought my attention back to him when he asked, "Are you willing to make the changes within the community?"

"I'm willing to do what's right for everyone."

He studied me, then nodded once.

There was a knock on the door. Nate drew in a breath and then opened it. Ezra strode in and came back to my side. He even snapped at Selma, who let out a frightened noise. I kept my smile from blooming. Some vampire she was. While I patted Ezra's head, I watched a wide-eyed Eric step through the entrance.

"Ah, hey."

"Eric, come down here please." I motioned to my end of the table. He did, looking at everyone suspiciously.

"What's going on?" he asked. Grace gasped. I wasn't sure if it was over Eric being human or how he didn't follow protocol by addressing me properly.

I didn't answer him. Instead, I addressed the rest of the room. "First order of business. As the new queen, I appoint new advisers at my side. Most I trust with my life, others will earn my trust in time. Nate, Alex, Asher, Thorn, Alma, Clyde, Michael, and Eric."

"What?" Odin screeched.

"You can't do this!" Barrett screamed.

"How dare you!" Grace spat.

It was only Selma who stayed silent with a bland look upon her face.

"I'll be organizing a meeting for tomorrow, a full-court announcement." I glanced to Thorn.

He bowed and said, "I'll make it happen, my queen."

"Thank you. For now, the four of you are excused."

"He's a human. He doesn't know our ways. This is blasphemy," Odin called.

"It doesn't matter what he is. I don't have to explain the reasons behind my choices. Now, please leave."

"It's not the end of this—" Barrett started, until Odin reached out and touched his back. Then he shut up and stormed from the room. Odin and Grace glared at us, then followed Barrett out.

Selma stood slowly. She looked to Clyde and rose a brow. He stared back, but I couldn't read anything from his expression. She laughed, shrugged, and then swayed her hips as she started behind me. I didn't miss the way her eyes ran over Asher or the small touch she skimmed over his shoulders.

In seconds, I had her by the throat and slammed into the wall. "Never touch what is *mine*," I snarled in her face.

She smiled. "I was just testing how strongly you felt for your mate. I could have had some fun with him."

"Never," I bit out. "Try testing me again and you won't live another day."

Her hands came up. "Yes, my queen. My apologies."

I tightened my hold for a moment longer and then dropped it, stepping back. Selma straightened her tight dress and walked from the room. I wanted to rip her head from her shoulders because she was still smiling.

It wasn't until Asher moved in behind me and ran his hands from my shoulders, down my arms, and then to my waist that I relaxed.

"You have made some enemies today," Clyde commented.

Opening my eyes, I stared at him. "Will you be one of them?" Had I made the right choice? I didn't have a clue what a queen was supposed to do, but my demand was spontaneous, and as soon as the words left my mouth, it felt right. Of course second-guessing myself would be something I'd do because there was a lot of weight on my shoulders. Hell, it all freaked me out, but I tried my best to keep if from showing. It would be something a queen did, right? Hide her emotions, act noble, at least try to.

I wanted to grab Thorn's shirt, drag him close and yell, "Am I doing the right thing? Do I sit like this? Do I look like I'm pulling this off, acting all queenish?"

Before I could do it though, Clyde spoke. "No, my queen." His lips tipped up into a close-mouthed smile. I would have to wait and see if he spoke the truth, or ask Nate if he could smell it. Clyde continued, "I agree with the changes you've made and look forward to seeing what you will bring the people."

"Peace. Safety. Fun times," Alma voiced. We all looked to her as she clapped her hands together. I could only hope whatever she knew or had seen was right. "May I also suggest one other for your advisers?"

"Who?" I questioned. My interest kept my wayward thoughts at bay, which was good.

"Agatha Delmar. She is a fine young witch."

I glanced at Thorn. He nodded. "She is the one who placed the spell on me to have me at your side when your powers surfaced."

"What's this?" Clyde asked.

Alma waved his question away. "You'll know all soon enough." A knock sounded on the door. Nate huffed but opened it. A woman, actually she looked to be in her late teens, came through. I wondered how old she really was. Alma laughed. "Right on time, Aggie."

The girl blushed. Her eyes met the floor before she bowed at the waist. "My queen."

Asher gently applied pressure to my waist. Right, I was supposed to say something. "Rise, Agatha." She did, but still didn't look me in the eyes. "Would you like to be another adviser to me?" Just because Alma suggested her or had "seen" her, didn't mean I wouldn't give the girl a choice. There was no doubt that allegiance to me could be dangerous. She had to make the decision herself. "I can't promise being one of my advisers will be safe. This also goes for everyone in the room." I took a moment to make eye contact with every-one. "Just because I said your name earlier doesn't mean you have to stay as an adviser. I didn't think before. I jumped ahead once more."

Thorn opened his mouth to say something, but I held up a hand. "Please, all of you think about it. I know my role won't be safe, and I don't want you risking your life just to help me."

Clyde stood and bowed. "Thank you for your concern, my queen."

I nodded. "All of you have until tomorrow. I will ask at the court meeting if you wish to stay as my adviser. I won't hold anything against you if you don't wish to."

"Good idea, my queen," Thorn stated. "If we announce who will remain as your advisers, it will show the people who they're able to seek for an ear with the queen."

"Should we worry about the old advisers?" Nate asked.

Clyde replied. "It would be best to keep an eye on them and who they speak with."

"Can we really speak freely and trust everyone in here?" Agatha asked, her gaze flicked to Clyde. He straightened and glared.

Alma waved her hand in the air. "It's fine, dear. Trust them all. You have my word."

It was good to hear her say that, especially when I wasn't fully convinced of Clyde myself. However, a little of that tension eased from me at Alma's words. And how did I know I could trust Alma? Because I could *feel* it, sense it. She was like a safe, warm grandmother who everyone wished they had.

"I… um…," Agatha started. When everyone looked at her, she blanched and shifted her gaze back to the floor. Then mumbled, "N-no one knew Marsala, I mean the former queen, and I were friends. I could, ah, be a secret adviser, find out things on the inside."

"You would be willing to do this?" I asked. She nodded straight away. Alma was also nodding.

"Grace is your coven mistress. You would go behind her back?" Clyde asked.

Her head lifted, and she glared at him. "I will never follow that woman's rules if it's the last thing I do."

Grace must have done something to piss Agatha off.

"Agatha, if she found out...."

"She won't. Not until she had to. Not until she knew... if, I mean, I would be under your protection, yes?"

"Of course," I said instantly.

She nodded. "Thorn has many men in the guard he trusts. Many men to protect us all. I know I'll be safe."

"Okay, Agatha, if this is what you choose to do." She seemed determined, and I had a feeling if I didn't agree and give my protection, she would do it anyway.

"Thank you, and please call me Aggie."

"Good, good," Alma called. "Aggie must go now before she's seen by too many."

Aggie bowed quickly and then slipped from the room.

"My queen, if you allow me, I'll seek out Michael and make the offer of adviser to him," Clyde offered.

"That would be good, thank you," I said. He bowed and left the room.

"It also reminds me, Michael needs a doctor for his mate. Would I be pushing it asking for the doctor the witches use?" I asked the rest of the room.

Nate stepped forward. "I have medical training."

"No," I blurted. Asher chuckled at my back. Alex and Thorn were also smiling. Ezra even let out a huff. Alma smiled wide, while Eric looked confused. I ran a hand over my face. "Sorry, but, ah, for the woman's safety, it would be better if it was anyone but one of you."

Nate rolled his eyes but said no more. I didn't miss the twitch on his lips, though.

"Now that changes are in the works, I'll tell Divina she'll be allowed to see anyone she wants. She's a ghoul who was previously a doctor. She's happy to help anyone but has been restricted because of the fool advisers getting in the former-queen's ear, trying to run things like the council does for control over the community. Poor Marsala was tired of the bickering back and forth. She knew her time was limited. She wanted to spend it in harmony with her mates. So she gave them too much free rein, and it went to their heads. But things are changing already for the better." Alma clapped; it seemed she loved to clap. She got to her feet slowly. "It's been a pleasure to meet you, Queen Paige Alice. I look forward to the times to come. Stay strong and believe in yourself and your mates."

"Thank you, Alma."

She dipped her head and left the room. It fell silent after Nate closed the door. I then glanced at Eric and said, "I've changed my mind. I don't think you should be an adviser for me. I won't risk your life or Yasmin's."

"But—"

I shook my head. "I know I probably won't change these stubborn asses' minds." Chuckles surrounded me. "And I know you can be stubborn, but I also know you'll do anything for your family. Yasmin and the kids need to stay safe. You're already at risk for being my family. I won't add to it."

He sighed and ran a hand through his hair. "I understand. Still, you'll need to give me something to do."

"There's plenty of jobs around. I'll bring some that are open to you tomorrow morning," Thorn suggested.

"Thanks." Eric nodded. "I better get back before Yasmin gets worried."

"Ezra, can you escort him please?"

Ezra nudged my hand. He knew I was sending him to protect Eric, and I knew Ezra would do anything for me. After they left, I turned to the men and said, "Can we head back and talk in my room?" Already I was tired of being around others. I just wanted the men and me alone.

"Of course," Asher replied.

CHAPTER SEVENTEEN
NATE

My eyes were on Paige's ass the entire walk back to her room. It was a good distraction to keep me from hunting those prejudice pricks down and ripping them a new asshole. But fuck, Paige had handled the situation perfectly. It was a good thing I'd gone for the tighter boxers, else everyone would have seen the hard-on I had for her and her assertiveness.

Christ, I even got off on her taking that bitch Selma to the wall to stake her claim over Asher.

Why did I fight the bond?

At that moment, I didn't have a clue.

Being the last one through her door, I took the time to adjust my dick behind my jeans. Paige went straight for the couch near the fire. I closed the door behind me and turned back to see Asher and Thorn sitting on each side of her. Alex moved and took the seat opposite them. I grabbed the last one beside him. I'd honestly been surprised when my wolf or I didn't feel threatened by the other men in the room when it came to Paige. My wolf huffed, like I was an idiot and missing something. Maybe it was because we knew she'd need more than one mate. We'd already accepted them into our pack to protect what was ours.

She needed all the help she could get. She acted like the queen well enough in front of others, but I could also scent— and it worried me others would as well—how she was unsure of everything. We had to remember it was all new to her. It was like she took on the job easily, but it wouldn't have been for herself. She was scared still. She did it for the people. She had a damn heart of gold, and I knew I wasn't the only one who worried it'd get her hurt in the end. Alex, Asher, and Thorn showed their concern over her in their own looks or actions. Still, we'd have her back through it all and hope with time she'd fully accept her title as queen.

Paige broke the silence by asking, "Why would they live like this? It's so... old fashioned, judgmental, arrogant."

"People don't like change. No matter what race," Asher explained.

"They've been this way for a very long time. From what I've gathered, the former queen, Marsala, new the battle would be too big for her," Thorn explained.

"And it's not for me?" Her brows dipped in worry.

Thorn reached for her hand. Their fingers twined together, and he rested them on his thigh. "She never wanted to believe her advisers would go against her, but Alma saw how Marsala wanted to change things. She also saw Marsala's death before the time was right. Before she could reach you. If that happened...." He shook his head. "Life for our society would have worsened."

"So she waited for me because they saw I would bring change and succeed? But in the process, how many will get hurt?"

"We can't worry about what will happen," I told her. "We just need to make sure to have each other's backs."

Her eyes looked glassy; it freaked me out.

"Or you all could leave and—"

"It's not happening," I clipped. I ground my teeth together.

She was foolish if she thought we would leave her to deal with everything on her own.

"But—"

"No buts. We're here, we're staying whether you like it or not."

She glared up at me. It was better than the fearful look in her eyes. "If you keep interrupting me, I won't like you staying."

I snorted and rolled my eyes.

Asher's arm went behind her, his hand around her neck. She glanced at him. "This is our destiny. You were meant to become queen, and we were meant to be by your side. Whatever is to come, the good, the bad... we will deal with it all together."

Wasn't that what I said? Although, Asher said it more eloquently. His way had Paige smiling softly up at him, her leaning into him, and his arm circling around her waist. Thorn didn't care. He kept holding her hand while she rested into Asher. I was surprised jealousy didn't rear its ugly head inside me.

Then again, this was how it was supposed to be.

She was made for all of us.

My resolve lowered, wavered. I didn't think I was completely interested in being Paige's, but I couldn't stop thinking about her. Claiming her, sinking my teeth into her flesh while I fucked her hard.

Fucking hell, my dick strained against my jeans.

I wasn't ready to finalize the bond, though. I'd wait, fight for her, and spend time around her. Make sure this bond would be the best choice for both of us, as well as the rest, in the end. Asher, Thorn, and Alex were completely for it. I could tell, and I was sure she knew it as well. She wasn't sure about me, and that was fine. I liked what we had. I liked fucking with her to bring her attitude out. I also wanted to wait until after the challenge. If shit happened to me, she wouldn't be too hung up should I fail. That was what I hoped anyway.

"It's nearing midnight. How about you try and rest," Thorn suggested.

She shrugged and sighed. "I suppose. Plus there will probably be a shitstorm tomorrow at the meeting, so I better be on top of my game."

I could definitely use more rest and some damn food.

"Do you have guards for her door or are we taking turns?" I asked.

"I'll call my brothers-in-arms. I trust them completely to guard her rooms."

"Wait," Paige called, her eyes widening. "What am I supposed to wear tomorrow?"

Another snort left me. She gave me the finger, and my lips twitched. Yeah, she would be feisty in bed, and I looked forward to that day, but it wouldn't be soon, even if my dick hated me for it.

"It will be formal clothing for such a gathering, Paige," Thorn told her.

She bit her bottom lip before saying, "But I don't have anything with me."

Asher glided a finger across her jaw. Her eyes darkened as they swung to him. "You have Alex. He can magic anything you desire."

Her gaze flared and swung to Alex, who smiled shyly and nodded. "It would be a pleasure."

"Thank you," she cried. "Could you conjure up some pajamas?"

"Easy." His eyes didn't even change color, but his cheeks pinked, and then he clicked his fingers.

"Ah, fuck." I groaned and scrubbed a hand over my face. "Time to go," I stated and stood. I grabbed Alex's arm and pulled him up.

"I didn't mean to do that. I thought of it briefly, but I wanted something else. I didn't mean it," he rambled as I pulled him toward the door. "Do you want me to change it?" he asked when I opened the door.

"No," Asher growled.

Just before I pulled Alex out of the room, I caught Paige look up to Asher as his eyes bled to green. Over my shoulder, I called, "Thorn, get those guards here."

"Yes." I heard him shift, his fingers pressing digits into a phone, but then closed the door and dragged Alex down to his room.

"You seriously had to go with that?" I asked, opening his door and walking in. I dropped his arm and made my way to the bed where I sat on the edge. My dick throbbed for release.

He threw out his hands. "I didn't mean it. It was a quick thought, and then I pictured something else, but my subconscious brought forward what I'd... ah...."

"Desired," I said.

He nodded.

Christ, if I had that power, I would have done the same. Her smooth, milky skin under that red lace was seared into my mind. She looked stunning. Absolutely fuckable.

"Do you think...?"

"Yes." I nodded. "Their bond will be finalized tonight." If I had stayed, I'd be a part of it too. We weren't ready, though.

"That's good, right?"

"It is. They want it. Paige does too, even though she's

scared of what it means." I glanced up from the floor to see Alex looking back to the door. "You'll get your chance. It'd be good for just the two of them though. All of us could overwhelm her."

"Yeah, you're right." He nodded again before meeting my eyes. "So you do want the bond?"

"Pretty sure. I'll see how things go."

Alex rolled his eyes. "You're going to wait until after the challenge in case anything happens. To try and save her some pain. But you know you're stronger than him, right?"

I hummed under my breath and shrugged. I wasn't so sure. I stood, needing to change the subject. "Anyway, can you click your fingers and get me some food?" I rubbed my gut.

Alex sighed. "Fine. I'm hungry as well." He made his way to a chair just as a tray of burgers and fries appeared on the coffee table in front of it.

"Perfect," I grumbled and dove for a burger. Three bites down and it disappeared. Another appeared, and I took that as well. Once I filled myself, I stood and stretched. "Gonna hit the shower and get some sleep." I headed for the bathroom.

Alex made a noise in the back of his throat. "In here? Again?"

"Yep," I replied without looking back.

* * *

Paige

I heard my door close after Nate and Alex and sensed Thorn stand and move away. He clipped some words into the phone, but I didn't hear what he said as I couldn't look away from

Asher. His green glowing eyes penetrated me. They also sent a shot of desire right to my breasts, causing my nipples to harden under the tiny red teddy Alex had put me in.

I would have laughed at Alex's choice and the shock that showed on his face when it happened, but wetness pooled between my legs, distracting me—as much as the vampire was right in front of me. Asher hissed out a breath. In the next second, I found myself on my back, bouncing on the bed, and Asher standing at the end of it. He shook his head, and the green haze receded. I got to my elbows and stared at him.

"Tell me to leave, Paige," he ordered darkly. When I didn't answer right away, his chest grumbled with a growl. His hand flashed out, and in the next moment, Asher gripped Thorn to his side by his shirt. "Tell *us* to leave, Paige," Asher demanded again.

I glanced from one man to the next, over and over. I couldn't seem to bring the words to my mouth.

I didn't want them to leave.

Was that crazy?

It was. It really was because I hardly knew them, yet I felt like I did. Felt like they were mine. *They are mine.* And they didn't seem to care I'd claimed them. In fact, both of them had voiced they wanted my claim and would be ready to take the next step to finalize the bond, at my pace. Right then, my pace was now.

They were my forever.

Meant to be with me, by my side, for the rest of our days.
Destiny.
Fate.
Made for each other.
Our lives had locked into each other's. Why would I deny

two men who had voiced their desire to be fully mine? I couldn't.

"Paige," Asher warned. "My strength is lessening."

That was good.

Thorn pried Asher's hand from his shirt. Though, I was sure Asher had hold of Thorn in the first place to keep himself in one place because, as soon as his hand unlatched, his eyes darkened and he pulled his shirt from his body.

"I can scent you, love. Tell me to leave," he snarled.

Love.

I liked he called me that. I kept my mouth closed and smiled slowly. Thorn chuckled. "Sweetheart, would you like me to step out?" He would leave if I wished it, which said a lot about the man.

Asher went to grab Thorn again. Maybe he thought to throw Thorn my way and make a run for it. He was probably concerned I wouldn't want this. However, Thorn sidestepped. Asher grumbled in the back of his throat, his fingers to his pants, and he undid the button.

I glanced to Thorn and could see the pronounced bulge behind his pants. Just like Asher's.

A pulse of lust swept through me. Asher's eyes flashed green and then back to his normal light blue, and his fangs peeked out. As Thorn's eyes hooded, he ran a hand over his face and shook out his body.

"Are you both sure—"

"Yes," Asher clipped.

"God, yes," Thorn replied on a groan. He grabbed his shirt at the back of his neck and tugged it free from his glorious body.

How did I get so lucky?

Oh wait, I remembered. I died, was reborn a ghoul, and

the queen's power got transferred to me, and then met my mates. Funny thing was, I would do everything again if it left me in the position I was in.

With two of my mates in front of me, both seeming ready to seal the deal.

Sitting, and then getting to my knees, I said, "Come here, my mates." The possession, the endearment, the truth of my words settled in my chest. Feeling right.

I let out a squeak when Asher flashed to my left side, kneeling on the bed. His hands distracted me—one touched my back, the other my waist where he gripped my teddy. My body shuddered. I didn't know Thorn had climbed onto the bed to my right side until his lips were on my shoulder. I sighed contentedly. My head arched to the side and Thorn trailed his tongue up to my neck and kissed there.

Asher lifted a hand from my back to slide my strap down from my other shoulder where he too kissed. I gasped from the pleasure both of them sent right to my core. Having their attention, both of them at the same time, was nearly over-whelming but absolutely needed. Wanted.

If this was too soon, I didn't care. They were mine. I could feel it in my heart, my soul.

I reached out to them, to their erections straining behind their clothes. Both of my men let out a sound as soon as I touched them. Asher thrust his into my hand, while Thorn let me take my fill as I ran my hand up and down his long, thick length.

The next second, I was facing Thorn with Asher pressing against my back. I glanced over my shoulder and raised my brows. He shook his head. "I love your touch, but having more of it will make this night over for me."

Thorn chuckled. Asher glared at him, and when he looked

back to me, he saw my thinning lips as I tried not to giggle. He growled, gripped my hair, and tugged my head back into his shoulder. A moan escaped me when his free hand slid to my waist and then up to cup my breast.

"Asher," I whispered.

"Ah, now who's losing it?"

I pouted. "Not fair."

"But you shall enjoy it." I heard a tear and felt a breeze hit my chest. I glanced down to see Asher had exposed my breasts. Thorn's lust-filled gaze caught my attention. "I think these beauties need attention, Thorn." Asher gripped one in each hand and gently caressed them.

"I think you're right, Asher."

While Asher ran his hands down over my stomach and slowly rocked his hardness into me, Thorn cupped both breasts and leaned in to suck the right nipple into his warm, wet mouth. I whimpered as he twirled my hard nipple around his tongue. "Thorn," I gasped and felt his smile against me.

When Asher's hand snuck inside my panties and held my mound, I moaned his name.

"Yes, my love?"

"Please."

"What do you need?"

His touch inside of me... but even more I needed his teeth biting into my flesh. The thought of it had me leaking more.

"Paige?" he clipped, sliding his fingers under my panties and over my lower lips.

Thorn bit down on my other nipple. I cried out and forced my breast into his face.

"My queen," Asher called low.

"Bite me, Asher," I ordered. He stilled at my back, his hand frozen in my panties.

"Love?"

"I need your fangs, Asher. Drink from me, please."

He sucked in a sharp breath. "Paige—"

I rocked my pussy over his hand and begged, "Please."

"Are you really going to leave our mate waiting?" Thorn asked, pressing a kiss on my breast before straightening. Mesmerized, I watched him undo his jeans. Asher must have been looking too because Thorn sent a wink over my shoulder. He stood from the bed and pushed his pants down his legs before standing and kicking them off. His dick sprang up and ready. Before I could take a good look at him, he climbed back on the bed. His grip moved to my waist. I snuck a hand down to take hold of him, but he clutched it, laughing. "Not yet, sweetheart."

Sweetheart.

I loved that as much as I loved it when Asher called me love.

I stilled as Asher tugged my long hair away from my neck. His tongue traced from my shoulder up to just below my ear where he gently nibbled before he whispered, "I would do anything for our queen, but especially our mate."

My body shuddered from his warm breath washing over my skin. When Thorn moved closer, my eyes lifted as he dipped his head and captured my lips with his. I moaned into his mouth when it opened, and our tongues tangled. He tasted and felt divine. Needing more contact, I ran my hands over his smooth skin.

Thorn fell back cursing. "Why did you push me?" he demanded from Asher. There was no answer; instead, Asher picked me up and set me, with my legs spread, over Thorn's waist.

Thorn's eyes widened, then lowered, and a grunt escaped

him when Asher reached between us and shred my panties with his claws.

"Are you ready, my love?" he growled into my ear.

For what I wasn't sure, but I was ready for anything they would both deliver. "Yes," I whispered.

With his arm around my waist, Asher pulled me back flush against his chest, grinding his cock against me. "Take him while I feed," he ordered harshly, lust dripping from his rough voice.

Nodding, I lifted to my knees, reached down, and with Thorn's help, we placed him against my entrance.

"Fucking stunning," Thorn rumbled, running his hands up my thighs.

"She is, and she's ours," Asher stated darkly. His claws on my waist dug in, but not enough to hurt me. The noise from his chest, which vibrated against my back, was possessive. He raked his fangs over my neck and then struck. A gasp fell from my mouth, and a moan soon followed when Thorn thrust up inside me. I closed my eyes as bliss soaked into me. Asher pulled my blood into his mouth. He groaned as he took his fill as Thorn hissed low, then both paused. They stilled.

Something built inside me. It warmed my stomach, spread up to my chest, and aimed to where I was connected to Asher and lower where Thorn was planted inside me. My men grunted, their grips tightening, Asher's around my waist and Thorn's on my hips.

The warmth heated more, and they moaned. It seared into me, and I cried out, but as soon as it flamed to pain, it disappeared. Opening my eyes, I gasped. The room glowed with Thorn's and Asher's gazes; their other selves had made an appearance. I saw it and felt it with their claws scraping against my skin. Asher withdrew his fangs and licked my sensitive skin. I shuddered and felt Thorn twitch inside me. I bit my bottom lip and rocked down on him, drawing out his growl.

My back arched, a cry escaping my lips, and both men grunted. Lust, desire, need, want, and even love shone through me, consumed me, and I could tell those emotions weren't only my own.

I could *feel* them.

Feel their emotions.

Did that mean they could feel mine?

"Yes," Asher said against my shoulder before he kissed me there. "The connection has been completed. You're mine."

"And mine," Thorn clipped as his hands trailed up to cup my breasts. He lifted his hips into me, and I moaned. "Watch who takes you, my queen."

Asher's hands at my waist lifted me a little to my knees. It gave Thorn access to pump his hard, warm length in and out of me. "Open your eyes, sweetheart," he ordered. I hadn't even realized I'd closed them, having dropped my head back onto Asher's shoulder, lost in the sensation.

Opening my eyes, I dropped my head to meet Thorn's heated gaze. He thrust up again, and my mouth dropped open. His love washed over me. It had my heart beating double time, had me returning that love and comforting both of us. When I ground down onto him, my power sprang forward, and I felt my eyes change and sensed how he thought it was beautiful.

"You're mine," I snarled. Asher gently pushed at my back, and I lowered my chest to Thorn's and rode his cock. "*Mine*," I bit out again.

"Yes, my queen. I'm yours," Thorn stated with delight in his tone. His hand threaded through my hair. He tugged me closer and captured my mouth. A hand slid between us. Asher. He rubbed a finger over my slickness and then on my clit. I moaned against Thorn's mouth. Content they didn't shy away from touching me when I had someone else inside me, it made me think of them together, of them kissing, touching, and tasting one another.

Thinking it, my belly swirled. Thinking it added more wetness that coated Thorn's cock.

Both of them growled deeply.

Thorn's mouth tore from mine. He cursed and groaned. Gripping my hair tightly again, he asked, "What did you just think of to send that amount of arousal our way?"

Heat hit my cheeks, and I glanced away, but Thorn brought my gaze back down to his when he pinched my nipple.

"It must have been good," Asher said roughly behind me. His hands ran over my back, my ass, where he slapped a cheek. "Tell us, love."

"You two. Together."

For a fraction of a second, they stilled, until Thorn rubbed up into me. "You don't mind if we do?"

I shook my head quickly. "It would turn me on. Seeing it and feeling the emotions when it happened... it would be a pleasure," I panted.

"One day soon, love. I would take any of your mates on in the bedroom if they allowed it," Asher said, his voice thicker. It had me moaning and rocking harder down on Thorn.

Thorn nodded. "I would enjoy anything from any of them."

Asher's finger sped up on my clit. My walls tightened around Thorn, causing him to hiss.

"Oh God," I cried out, losing myself to the sudden

orgasm. Thorn growled deeply within his chest as he pulled me back down, claiming my mouth. I whimpered into it, still climaxing around him. He grunted, "Coming," and kissed me roughly as he throbbed and warmth filled my insides.

Thorn's hold relaxed. Asher must have seen it because next I was losing Thorn from within and was up on my knees. A scream tore from my throat when Asher embedded himself straight into me. Another climax overwhelmed me. Thorn held me while Asher fucked me hard and fast.

I loved every second of it.

Asher leaned over me, still drilling his hips, his cock pistoning in and out of me as he bit my shoulder. He growled, wrapping his arms tightly around my chest. I didn't think it possible, but another orgasm had me crying his name.

He hissed, withdrew his fangs and licked over the spot, still while I kept coming. He snarled, and I felt his longer length surge inside once more as he spilled his seed inside me.

A purring noise had me turning my head slightly to see Asher's eyes glowing. He pulled back his hips and slowly pushed back in.

"*Mine*," he grunted, his vampire riding his voice.

"Yes." I breathed the word.

His gaze shifted to Thorn under me. "*Ours*."

Thorn nodded. "Yes, our mate, and let's take care of her."

The purr in Asher's chest didn't subside as he pulled out. It continued as he lifted me from the bed into his arms. Thorn slowly climbed from the bed and went into the bathroom. Once out of sight, I heard flowing water.

Asher rubbed his cheek against mine, then pressed his nose in my neck and inhaled deeply.

When Thorn came back into the room, Asher growled

low, and I linked an arm around his shoulders. Thorn stilled. "Ours remember."

Asher grunted and went back to purring. His vampire sent his pleasure, his happiness out to me. He loved me, loved that I was his mate, and I knew Thorn felt the same.

We'd completed the bond. I was theirs as much as they were mine, and I felt giddy from it. A laugh rumbled out of my vampire, while Thorn smiled brightly.

The fear over forcing them into the situation fell away. We all wanted to be here, be with one another, and be each other's forever.

After all, it was meant to be.

And I looked forward to finalizing the bond with my other mates.

CHAPTER EIGHTEEN

NATE

By the time I got out of the bathroom, which took me longer than normal since I had a hard-on to deal with, Alex sat on the bed with a book in hand dressed in nothing but boxers. *Alex.* He'd been Smith for so long, and yet here he was Alex. It felt right. Better even.

The room was only lit by the lamp beside him on the small table. Even without that I could see clearly in the dark thanks to my animal.

"Need boxers," I told him. Without looking, he clicked his fingers, and under my towel, I felt a new pair of boxers. I dropped the towel and glanced down. The boxers were tighter than usual and silk. I raised a brow at Alex, but his gaze was on the discarded towel on the floor. A tick started in his jaw while a grin popped up on my lips. I knew the guy was a clean freak, but I now understood it was worse. I gave him time to see how long it took for him to either deal with it or say something. I'd made it to the other side of the bed before the towel disappeared with another click of his fingers.

His attention returned to his book. "It's hanging in the bathroom."

A laugh escaped me as I climbed under the sheet. What was weird was that it felt normal. It wasn't strange, which didn't really make sense because it was Alex. A man I'd worked alongside for years. Out of the corner of my eye, I studied him while I settled back to lie flat with my arms behind my head. I didn't know what he was reading, but he was engrossed in it. His eyes flicked over the words quickly, and he turned page after page as I kept staring. I'd never noticed how fit he was or the fact he smiled to himself while reading. How his face lit up at certain spots in the book.

But why was I noticing now?

He was damn young compared to me and Asher. It showed a lot, but he still held his own. He was strong and fast with his magic. Not only that, but in body as well, which explained the six-pack I currently stared at.

Christ, why was I eyeing him up?

Was the connection to Paige the reason? If so, it would at least explain why my dick suddenly twitched as I ran my eyes over him. Though, it could have to do with the way he bit his bottom lip, the way his eyes widened and then hooded as he read on.

Then it hit me.

Something in the book had turned him on.

"What're you reading?" I asked to the quiet room.

Alex jumped; he even threw the book. "Nothing!" he shouted. He took a gulp of air. "Jesus, I thought you'd crashed, Nate. You been awake this whole time?"

"Yep."

He leaned out of bed, picked up his book and grumbled, "Go to sleep." He opened the book again, finding the page he was on and started reading again. Another wave of arousal hit my senses. My dick didn't care it was a guy it stood to attention for behind the boxers, ready for action. I sucked in a big breath, drawing in his scent more, and Alex's wide eyes snapped down to me. "What are you doing?"

I smirked. "Wanting to know what you're reading that's

turning you on." I made a grab for the book, but he threw it across the room, then clicked his fingers, and it disappeared.

"I'm not... t-turned on."

I drew in another breath.

"Stop that," he demanded, scowling down at me with the color of fire over his cheeks. He slid down in the bed and turned off the light.

Rolling to my side, my eyes adjusted to the darkness and brought the room into clear focus. My wolf paced inside me. He wanted some action in any way he could. Fight or fuck.

"What were you reading, Alex?"

He sighed and rested an arm over his face. "A book," he mumbled.

"And it turned you on?" My tone was deeper, rougher.

He groaned in agitation. "Can you just drop it?"

"No."

"Fine. Yes, it turned me on, but I always seem to be aroused since Paige, ah, claimed me."

I snorted. "I know the feeling." I paused, letting him think the conversation was over. Then said, "What were you reading?"

He cursed under his breath. "Normal words."

"Normal words got you hard?"

He made a noise in the back of his throat. "I'm *not* hard. Just... I was... aroused. *Now,* can we drop it?"

I couldn't because my wolf and I liked teasing him, liked seeing him flustered and his cheeks tinted. Even more, we liked the thought of knowing Alex was hard. It shocked me for a second, but it also aroused us. With a quick movement, I reached out and gripped his erection. He cursed again, then yelled, "What the hell?"

"You're lying to me, Alex," I clipped. I didn't like he lied.

I didn't like he hid it. What I did like was the weight of his erection in my hand. I ran my palm up and down. He gripped my wrist to stop me. I growled low, and he stilled.

"W-What are you doing?"

I wasn't sure. I'd never felt another guy's junk, but I was, and hell, it wasn't too bad. I enjoyed the way his voice hitched. I didn't want him to make me stop. The thought of stopping annoyed me and my wolf. So I didn't answer him; instead, I peeled his hand off my wrist and dragged it down to cover my hard dick. His breath picked up. Another shot of desire hit the room. I drew it in, and a rumble escaped from my mouth. I rocked into his hand while I ran mine up and down his length. His breath hitched again.

"Nate," he whispered. Yeah, he liked this. He wanted to touch me, and he wanted *my* touch. Fuck, that pleased me and my wolf.

"No," I bit out.

"You're touching me." His low, needy voice had me leaning in and nipping his shoulder.

"And you're touching me," I said roughly. He hadn't stopped touching me, even when I'd removed my hand. In fact, he was rubbing me up and down slowly. My wolf let out a rumble; he suddenly felt smug.

"But... we... should stop."

"No," I clipped harshly. His hand stopped for a moment, and I saw him look my way.

"Your eyes are glowing, Nate."

I knew they were. My wolf was close. He wanted more. He wanted to control. Not me, but *he* wanted *me* to control Alex. Hell, I even liked the idea of it. With a deep, rumbling growl, I gripped Alex and twisted him enough so I could rub my dick into his ass cheeks. The gasp that dropped from his lips jerked my dick hard. I pulled him back and ground my dick into him.

"Nate," he half warned, half breathed.

Another growl radiated out of my chest when he went to move away from me. He stilled.

"Just… wait. For a moment, let go," Alex said.

I didn't like it. My wolf really didn't want to, but I forced my hands to loosen. Alex managed to slip out of my grip. He flung the blanket back, and I thought he was getting out of bed. I made a grab for him when he quickly said, "Wait." It was only his heated eyes that had me stilling and waiting.

His eyes told me he wouldn't be stopping this.

He got to his knees beside me. A hiss escaped me when he clicked his fingers, and a tube of lube appeared on the bed. At the same time, our boxers disappeared. I could have come right there and then.

Mine. Ours. My wolf sounded in my mind and then threw me images of Paige, Alex, Asher and Thorn. *Ours.* He snarled with another picture of me and Paige together.

Fuck me. It all made sense now—why we'd been accepting of the other men.

The wolf saw everyone as Paige and mine.

He wanted to claim all of them as well. Like Paige did.

Ours.

Alex sat back on his calves, his erection jutting out. He was hard for me. Hard because I'd been touching him.

"Did I read this moment wrong?" he asked, and even in the dark I could see the hesitant look in his eyes as well as the blush coating his face and neck. He shook his head and went to move, but I grabbed his arm.

"You ever done this…?" I asked.

"With a guy? Once."

Fuck, why did I want to hunt that one guy down and rip his dick off to shove it down his throat? My wolf didn't like it either. Another growl erupted and kept rumbling from my chest as I got to my knees, slipping in behind him. "No more," I snarled.

"S-Sorry?"

I didn't say anything. Instead, I ran my hands down over his shoulders, his back. His skin under my touch, smooth and warm, appeased my wolf. I nipped at his shoulder. An image of me biting him touched my mind.

Claim, my wolf and I thought together.

With a hand to his shoulder, I pushed him forward. He went to his hands, his ass rising for me. My chest vibrated with a deep guttural sound. I ran a finger over his hole. On contact, his hips jerked forward. I pulled him back with a hand to his thigh.

He wouldn't take away from me what he was offering. "Mine," I bit out. The sound in my chest didn't stop. I grabbed the tube of lube. Even though my wolf wanted me embedded deep inside Alex, I knew I had to take my time.

"Yes," Alex whispered.

Yes? He knew he was mine?

My lips tugged up.

I lathered my fingers, his ring, and my dick in a lot of lube before throwing the bottle to the bed again. When I ran my fingers over his ring again, he whimpered. When I pressed one inside, he gasped. I joined another with the first, watching my fingers work his hole, stretching it. We didn't need protection. Neither of us could get any human diseases, which I was goddamn grateful for because my dick was already leaking at the thought of being inside him with nothing between us.

"Should... should I worry about your growls? Your dominance?"

Leaning down, I kissed his lower back. My chest wouldn't quit vibrating over the sound my content wolf made. He knew I was going to get what we wanted. He was happy.

Kissing his waist, I trailed my tongue up to his shoulder where I nipped again. "Probably."

When I pressed my fingers deeper, rubbing against what I was sure was his prostate, he threw his head back and moaned.

"Later," he muttered. Then after a few beats, he snapped, "Nate."

"You want me inside?"

He glared over his shoulder. "Yes."

My wolf howled inside me. As I forced his chest to the bed, I slipped my fingers free. He mewed in protest. I got to my knees and positioned myself behind him, gripping my leaking dick. I rubbed it up and down over him. He panted, and I saw him take a hand under him. His body moved slightly while he jerked his dick in his hand.

"Mine," I clipped, and reached for his arm. He let me pull it away from him. Stretching over his back, I pressed my cock at his hole. As soon as I inched in, I crouched and leaned into him more, holding his hands down on the bed.

I dragged my lips over his shoulder. Licking, tasting. With his head turned sideways, he opened his eyes, and I slammed deep inside. His mouth opened at the intrusion, his eyes darkening, and then he licked his lips.

Fuck me. He liked it.

Ours, my wolf chimed.

Slowly, I pulled out and then back in. Alex moaned. I grunted deeply.

Christ, he felt amazing. I buried myself as far as I could go and felt a tingle hit my spine.

"Nate?" Alex must have sensed something. He went to move but stilled when I growled menacingly.

He was ours.

My body grew. The half shift swept over me. My claws sprouted, along with my teeth. Alex gasped and rocked back onto me. My dick had grown, my pink tip would be out and deeper inside him.

"Mine," I snarled before moving back, gripping his hips and fucking him hard and fast. He took it all. He cried out, groaned, panted, and moaned for us.

"Nate," he called, and we knew he was close.

Still pounding into him, I grabbed his shoulder and dragged him up to his hands. With our increased height, we mounted him, jerking only our hips in and out while we lay over his back.

"Nate," he moaned again.

Our teeth latched onto his shoulder. We bit down, drawing blood. Immediately, he cried out and shuddered under us. Our bite deepened while his body kept shaking and coming. We growled around his skin. Our balls drew up, and finally, goddamn finally, our cum shot inside his ass as we moved in and out fast.

My wolf receded, sated. Carefully, I took my teeth out of Alex and licked the spot. I jerked inside him, the last of my cum squirting out. My claws, teeth, and body shrank down to my human form. Slowly, I withdrew. As if in a daze, Alex slumped forward, flat on his stomach. I moved to the side and brought him into me, curling my arms around him.

He yawned. "We'll talk about what happened in the morning."

I hummed under my breath, spent and tired. But damn happy since it seemed the bonding, not only with Paige, but with all of us, was underway.

* * *

Alex

When I woke, it was to the arm over my waist loosening and moving as Nate rolled to his back and then slid out of bed. I didn't open my eyes. Instead, my mind bombarded me with images of the night before. My body relished in the desire I'd experienced.

Never in my life would I have thought Nate and I would be in that situation.

Never.

Was I glad it happened? Yes. It felt right, good. That was if I didn't die of embarrassment first, and if I didn't, I would ask for it again. However, I knew I would never be good at dealing with the morning after with someone I'd just had sex with. Especially since it was something I hadn't ever experienced before. I either left or they did after the deed was done. So how did I act? Did we high-five? Tell each other good job? Go on like it never happened? I'd been with *one* other man and hadn't even stayed around after to worry about things like this. I'd also been with a couple of women, but those times weren't ones I stuck around for either. My studies, magic, and then work took up all of my time. I'd picked those people up at clubs and used them as a stress reliever, but I never looked for anything more.

I wondered if it was because I'd been destined for more.

For Paige.

For Paige and her men.

Heck, it wasn't that. I just wasn't the kind of guy who slept around. I enjoyed my own company. I didn't feel the need to seek out another being for pleasure when I could bring it on myself with my own hand... or fingers.

I heard the shower turn off. It was then I gasped and realized I should have used the time to get out of here. But then I remembered the room we were in was the one I'd been assigned. So instead, I sat up quickly and got out, standing beside it. I called up a spell to clean the sheets and make the bed.

Then I froze.

The bathroom door opened. Footsteps approached. Should I have turned and held out my hand for a shake? Worry churned my stomach. What would Paige think? Shit, she might not like what happened between us. We shouldn't have done it.

We had to hide it. No one could know.

Teeth nipping at my shoulder had me jolting on the spot. "Enough thinking," Nate ordered.

"I wasn't," I told him.

He snorted. "Sure. Explains why you're standing by the bed naked."

My eyes widened. I glanced down, and I *was* naked. With a click of my fingers, my body was clean, my hair was done, and a dark blue suit fitted my frame. Satisfied, I looked at Nate who... was... naked.

"I enjoy you looking, but we should get to Paige's," he said with a smirk because I *had* been running my gaze over him slowly.

Another click of my fingers and a black suit covered his amazing body. His brows dipped. "A monkey suit?"

I cleared my throat because he looked nearly as good in it as he was out of it. "Yes. We have to stand by Paige while she speaks with everyone. I don't think jeans will do it."

He sighed. "Fine." His jaw clenched.

"Ah… also, I don't think we should have done what we did last night. Paige might not like it, so we shouldn't, um, that's if you were thinking of doing it again… but we shouldn't do it again."

Oh shit.

Nate's lips thinned, his eyes narrowed, and his hands fisted at his sides. His nostrils flared. He stretched his neck, rolling his head around before lasering me with another glower. "It *should* have happened. It *will* happen again, and Paige *will* accept it," he clipped before storming to the door and opening it.

My power flared. I transported to the door and slammed it closed before he could step out. "Nate, listen to me. We—"

He crowded me, aligning his body with mine against the door. "What happened last night?"

The bite.

"Yes, about that—" I started.

"My wolf and I claimed you. We'll be claiming Asher, Thorn, *and* Paige. You're ours. What happened last night fucking rocked. I have a feeling it's because of Paige, because of her claim and power changing us all, but that doesn't matter because it happened. We deal, move on, and again, you're—"

He leaned in more and rubbed his nose against mine just before he pressed his lips against my own. Shock blasted through me. With wide eyes, I took in his own big gaze, until I saw his green eyes darken and lower, his body relaxing against mine. As if the kiss was the final moment in the claim. It was done. I *was* his and for the life of me, I couldn't find the fight in me anymore. Nor did I want to. Not when he nipped at my bottom lip playfully and then deepened the kiss. I lost control and grabbed him to me, molding and melting with him. When we finally came up for air, he growled out deep and low. "*Mine.*"

My heart hammered in my chest, and my breathing left me panting. Too stunned and moved to say anything, Nate was able to move me aside and open the door again. He walked out while I gripped my chest.

He had claimed me completely.

Me.

A mage to his shifter.

His wolf wanted me.

Me. Asher. Thorn and Paige.

My dick was still stuck on the fact he wanted it to happen again before I rushed out of the room after him.

CHAPTER NINETEEN
PAIGE

I sat on the couch eating a bagel with cream cheese. I had about two hours before I had to leave for the meeting I called. My body ached in the best of ways. There was no way I could wipe the smile off my face. In fact, I was looking forward to another night of testing out the bed once more. Whether it was with Asher and Thorn again, or one of them on their own. Even if it was with Nate, if I didn't kill him, or Alex… or both of them together.

My hormones had amped up more after the previous night, and I couldn't stop thinking about it or staring at the men who'd made my body sing. Thorn sat opposite me reading something on his iPad, while Asher had just come from the bathroom and stood near the couch I was on, drying his hair.

"If you keep thinking about last night or looking at me like that, love, we won't make the meeting."

"Okay." I smiled, still eyeing him and allowing them to feel my desire.

He laughed.

"Finish your bagel, sweetheart," Thorn said. He was already smirking my way when I glanced to him. He enjoyed the way I'd moaned over the first bite of bagel. His rush of arousal hit me from where he sat. However, I couldn't help that I was starving; they'd used all my energy up.

I took another bite and chewed slowly. Thorn's eyes hooded. He licked his lips, and somehow, I felt that over my clit. I rubbed my legs together under my robe, and Thorn's mouth tipped up.

Before things got carried away, I said, "Can I ask you both a question?"

Asher nodded once, as Thorn replied, "Of course."

"How, ah, how did you both become what you are? I mean, if it's not something you want to talk about, I understand…. I just, um, wanted to know more about you both."

Asher moved over to the couch and sat on the armrest. He nodded at Thorn, who smiled. "My story isn't exciting or anything. I was turned by one of the former queen's bonded mates. I'd been out one night drinking at a bar after a long day of work at my family's farm."

"You're a country boy?" I grinned.

Thorn smirked. "I was, yes. I have my cowboy gear in the back of my wardrobe if you would like to see it?"

Yes please. I nodded and knew he felt my excitement when he chuckled. "One night soon, sweetheart. Back to the story. There were a couple of men there who were hassling a woman. I told them to stop. They did, after some fists were exchanged with faces. They left, and I thought that would be the end of it. However, it wasn't. They were waiting outside of the bar and then shot me." I gasped, worry clutching at my chest. "I'm all right, Paige, as you can see." I could, but knowing he'd been shot didn't sit well. "Justice, the mate to the former queen, found me. He killed the men before he dropped to his knees beside me. We both knew I would die, but he asked if I wanted to live but become something else. He saw what had happened and knew I was a good man, but by living, I would have to leave the life I had behind."

"Your family."

"Yes. My choice was either death or to live on as something else. I picked something else after I made sure I would be able to keep an eye on my family from a distance afterward."

"Do you regret your choice?" I asked, feeling kind of afraid of his answer because it meant he didn't like where his life now was.

He shook his head quickly. "It cut me deeply, knowing my family thought me dead, but... now I know what my purpose is. To be by your side. I would have picked it again and again because it led me to be here with you."

Relief washed through me. "D-Do you still see them?"

"Sometimes. At least my great nieces and nephews. My parents and brothers are long gone. They lived, loved, and were happy. It was all I wanted for them."

"How did you become a guard for the queen?"

"Training, and a lot of it. Justice took a liking to me. He taught me everything I know, and I worked my way up." I opened my mouth to ask another question when Thorn held up his hand. "We have so much time to get to know each other completely, but I'm afraid this morning we don't have enough to go into a lot of it. If you would like to hear Asher's story, then we should move on to it."

He was right. We had so much time, and knowing it warmed me within. "Okay." I smiled and looked to Asher. His pinched brows and thinned lips had me reaching out to take his hand. "You don't have to tell me now or ever if you—"

"I wish to. Only my change isn't as honorable as Thorn's."

"You have to know by now that no matter what your past entailed, I'll still be by your side. I'll still love you for the man you've shown me, and that man is caring, protective, and fierce when he needs to be."

His brows shot up. "You love me?"

Shock had me jerking my head back. I thought they would have sensed it. "Well, yes. Both of you. Can't you feel it?"

His eyes darkened. "I can, but hearing the words means something as well."

"Agreed," Thorn stated, his voice thick and rough. A wave of love swept through me from both of them. It caused a frantic beat to my heart.

Asher's thumb gently stroked my skin as he started talking. "I had been called to my family's house for a dinner. They were aristocrats in the town we lived in and wanted to make a good impression on someone. At first, I told them I wouldn't because I'd not long moved out to get away from them. Yet, as soon as my father told me he would cut off my money, I went because I was selfish and liked the way I lived. No one knew of the existence of *others* in the world."

He licked his lips. "We learned differently that night. The couple my father invited were new to town but flaunted their money around, so he wanted to be the first to invite them over because he wanted our family to be the talk of the town. We found out exactly who they were after dinner. First, they killed my sister, then my mother. Lisa had taken a liking to me. She wanted to keep me as her pet." A growl dropped from my lips. Asher squeezed my hand. "It's fine, love. They got what they deserved in the end. Lisa started the process. I didn't know I would become what they were and wake with a hunger like I'd never felt." Pain danced on his features and had him thinning his lips. I knew why a second later when he said, "They left my father alive to be my first kill. I didn't know at the time who I was feeding from. Until it was too late. However, I didn't grieve his death or my family for a long time after because the hunger had taken over. I killed over fifty people before it was sated. It was a week later when I finally came back to myself."

"Is that what it's like for all vampires when they're first changed?"

He shook his head sadly. "If they have a kind master, they're taken care of, taught how to feed, how long for so no death will occur. Lisa and David didn't care. They wanted me to go on a rampage. They didn't realize their mistake until I took their lives. Nearly killing myself in the process because with Lisa being my master, I didn't know our connection could harm her younger children. If it hadn't been for Cynthia, a vampire who happened to be in the area, I would have died along with them. She saved me and taught me the rules, how we were supposed to live."

My anger for Lisa and David quickly shifted. Jealousy burned in my gut, but I had no right. I should have been grateful for Cynthia's help, else I wouldn't have Asher by my side.

Asher reached out and tucked my hair behind my ear. "She has been a long-time friend more than we were lovers. You have nothing to fear from her or my time. You are my world. Since the moment I laid my eyes on you."

Well… I couldn't say anything to that.

I nodded stiffly and rolled my shoulders back. "Okay," I clipped since my brain was still on the fact that they *had* been lovers. Asher chuckled. I looked at Thorn to find him smiling.

"Sweetheart, you'll now need to worry that we never cross any of your exes. I would kill them knowing they have touched you." His eyes tinted red before returning to normal.

Then I remembered. He'd said the possessiveness would

grow once the bond was complete. I laughed. "Welcome to my world, guys."

Both growled low, causing me to laugh again.

Maybe it would be best to move on from the subject altogether for now or we'd all end up angry. Although there was one thing I needed to make clear for Asher. Glancing up at him, I pushed my love into him. "You do know none of it is your fault."

"The guilt over killing innocent people will always live inside me. It was why I chose to work for the council so long ago. To help other newborns, to erase the existence of cruel masters, and to protect anyone I could."

How couldn't he see he'd paid his dues by doing so much good? Smiling, I told him, "One day I'll have you seeing the amazing man I see in front of me, Asher. And when you do, I hope it'll ease the guilt you still hold."

"Anything you wish, love."

He was only placating me, I knew it, but I gave it to him. My glower made him chuckle. I knew I wouldn't get anywhere today with making him see my reason, so I chose to move on. *For now.* "Do you think we can stop by Yasmin's and pick up Ezra on the way?" I missed my hellhound. He'd taken it upon himself to protect my family for me. It was sweet and very kind, but I did love having him at my side.

"Yes, of course," Thorn said.

"Speaking of him," Asher started, "how did it come about? Do you know why he was there when you woke?"

I shook my head. "I've never known how or why he came to me in the first place. How he even found me. But, for me, the reasons don't matter. I'll always be grateful and love him for it. He's mine and I'm his."

Asher and Thorn glanced at one another and shared a look I didn't understand. "What was that?" I asked.

"What, sweetheart?"

"You know what, that look."

"I'm not sure." Thorn smiled. "Are you hungry for more than a bagel?" he questioned, and it threw me because it had me wondering something.

"We'll get back to that look soon," I promised. "No, I'm not hungry for something *more* just yet. Soon though I'm sure. But I did just wonder where the 'food' came from."

"We have a certain group that visits the morgues close by. We also protect the area surrounding us from those looking to harm anyone in the society."

"Oh... well, there you go."

My door came open, and I saw Asher had already been looking that way before Nate strolled in and then Alex.

Alex, who was bright red in the face.

Alex, who somehow smelled different.

Alex, who looked everywhere but at anyone.

"Morning," I called.

Nate grunted, but there wasn't any heat behind it. Actually, I was sure that on his lips was a tiny smile. He moved differently, too. Instead of stomping, he was lighter on his feet as he made his way to the table with coffee and food on it. Which Thorn had delivered that morning. They both looked amazing and very edible in their suits. Like Thorn had after he'd gotten ready.

"Morning," Alex replied from where he stood near the door. He tugged at the neck of his shirt. I caught his throat moving when he swallowed thickly after Asher moved from the armrest and stepped close to him.

I glanced back to Nate, who stuffed his face with bacon.

In his other hand, he held up a bagel with nothing on it, ready to shove it in his mouth. He flicked his eyes to Asher and Alex. "Leave him alone," he said around his mouthful.

When Asher's wide eyes shot to Nate's, I knew I was missing something.

"What's going on?" I even looked at Thorn when no one replied to see if he knew anything. His brows nearly met his hairline, and he looked from Nate to Alex and back again.

I put the rest of my bagel on the plate and stood with my hands on my hips. "What's going on?"

"Nothing," Alex blurted quickly and loudly. His blush spread to his ears and down his neck.

At the same time, Nate, in a rough tone, said, "Alex and I slept together last night."

"Nate," Alex yelled.

Eyeing Nate, I replied, "So? You did that the night before as well."

His brows rose, and he gave me a look that said he thought I was stupid. I glowered at him.

"I. Fucked. Him," he stated slowly.

My mouth dropped open, my heart raced, and my eyes flared.

Nate and Alex.

Last night.

Nate was inside Alex.

In bed.

A wave of heat sank into my gut and moved lower to press inside me. I exclaimed, "You mean I missed out on seeing it?" I slapped a hand over my mouth. I couldn't believe I just said that when *they* didn't know it would turn me on. They hadn't been in the room last night. Instead, they'd been together. Dear God, I wanted to see that.

I heard Alex choke on a cough. I glanced to him to see he was having a hard time getting his redness under control while he tried to breathe normally. I spun my head back to Nate when, to my utter shock, he laughed aloud.

Once he settled and after we'd all watched him, he went back to rolling his eyes at us and glowering before taking a gulp of his coffee. Then I witnessed in astonishment as he made another cup and walked it over to Alex, who was still red in the face but also shocked by the kind gesture from Nate. Alex took the mug with shaky hands and muttered, "Thanks."

Nate shrugged and went back to the food.

After a while, Nate looked at us all. "For fuck's sake, what?"

"So…," I started. I honestly didn't know what to say. I did want *all* the details of the previous night, but I was sure if we spoke about it, Alex would have a heart attack. I quickly added, "Nothing."

Thorn cleared his throat to grab everyone's attention, "I don't think that's all that—"

"Can we just focus on the day, talk about that later?" Nate interrupted. His gaze met mine. "Do you know what you're going to say?"

To try and save his mood from going down to asshole land, I went along with his change of subject. "I'm going to wing it."

Everyone stared at me.

"Wing it?" Thorn asked.

"Well, yes."

"You don't have anything planned?" Alex queried.

"Nope." I shook my head. I picked my bagel back up and took a big bite.

"And she's the queen," Nate mumbled, but we all heard. I shot him the finger. Immediately, he chuckled. Yep, he was in a good mood. It told me all Nate needed was a fine night in bed with someone.... My body tensed. Not just anyone, though. I wouldn't, no, *couldn't* allow it. I would kill a person if anyone other than one of my mates or me touched him. Just the thought of it burned my stomach.

"Love, what's on your mind?" Asher asked as he walked to my side. Both he and Thorn would have sensed my emotions shift.

I glanced around. All my men were watching me. "Not much." At my side, he wrapped an arm around my waist. I leaned into him, and it helped calm the fire inside me.

A knock sounded on the door. Since Alex was near it, he opened it, and in stepped a man in his thirties. He bowed at me, but his eyes were on our mage. I bristled.

"My queen, Gregory asked me to come and see if there was anything else you needed."

"No, I'm fine."

"Can I do anything for anyone in here?" he purred. His gaze was right on Alex. I was about to tell him we were fine when something crashed Nate's way. I looked over and saw his cup on the floor, and he moved toward the male.

He shoved the man's chest hard.

"Nate," Alex admonished. I was too stunned to say anything.

"Look at him like that again, and I'll cut your eyes out and feed them to you. Now get the fuck out. We don't need anything."

The man paled. He bowed over and over and backed further out of the room. "Yes, sir. Sorry, sir." The fool looked over at Alex once more, and Nate dove for him, but Alex wrapped his arms around Nate, who struggled. Thorn got up and rushed to the door, slamming it closed after the man. He leaned against it.

"Calm the hell down," Alex ordered.

Nate stilled. He huffed and relaxed into Alex.

"What was that about?" I asked out of the corner of my mouth to Asher. I honestly found it quite arousing. Well, after the annoyance fell away since Nate took care of the problem.

"I think it's something we'll discuss after the conference today," Asher said.

Dang it. I didn't want to wait, but I had a feeling it could be a long talk. "Fine."

"Alex, could you do your magic on me and Asher?"

With a final look to Nate, who nodded, Alex smiled over at me and came my way. "It would be an honor."

CHAPTER TWENTY
PAIGE

Alex had dressed me in a simple long black dress and heels. My hair was in two braids, which I pulled over my shoulders. After Alex had done his work, I didn't want to leave the room with the way all the men had been staring at me. Even Alex and Nate. However, I knew if I started something, we would have been late or not gone at all. Which wouldn't look good since I'd organized this meeting.

We were surrounded by Thorn's buddy elite guards as we walked. Then Thorn was in front of me leading the way. Asher walked at my right side, with Nate on my left and Alex following close behind with Ezra beside him. Ezra had been in my sister's suite all night, and the way he sniffed all of us when we'd stopped in there, he knew exactly what had happened the previous night. He'd wheezed in his laughing way.

Yasmin and Eric wanted to attend, but I asked them to stay back for their safety. Eventually, Yasmin agreed when I brought the kids into it. Thorn had some of his men stay to guard them.

We stopped just outside the throne room. Thorn turned to me and asked softly, "Are you ready, my queen?"

I wasn't.

I didn't think I would ever be ready, but this was my new life, my responsibility, and one day it would fully sink in. I would completely accept my new role. For now, I was winging it and praying for the best. Although, with my mates at my side, it helped my confidence. Their unwavering support had *me* believing I could do this. Even when it scared me to a point where, if I still went to the bathroom, I would have shit myself quite a few times over.

I ran my hands down my dress, pushed all joking aside, and told myself once more that I was doing the right thing by accepting the knowledge of me being the ghoul queen.

For me, for my mates, and for our people who sought refuge against the council. I would be the best queen I could be.

Resting a hand against my hard-beating heart, I nodded. Thorn smiled before facing toward the double wooden doors. As soon as he did, two of his men in front opened the doors and stepped aside. At least ten others entered before we did.

I could hear the voices, the murmurs, the heartbeats. I could even scent the worry, the excitement, and the hate. It was an added bonus to becoming queen—at least that was what Thorn told me, and I trusted him completely. The power had been slowly manifesting.

The two mates I had finalized the bond with sent me calmness. It rolled into me, and I straightened, lifting my head high just as Thorn started into the room. With a slow pace, I followed, knowing my men would be with me every step of the way.

I blocked out what I could hear, what I could scent, and made my way down between pews. It took a while to reach the front since the room was so large, but eventually, I climbed the steps to the platform and stopped just in front of the throne.

Turning, I gazed out into the room. There were so many

people in attendance, standing and watching me. Waiting. I didn't say anything until my men were in position. Asher and Thorn took a spot on each side of me, just a step back from the chair. Alex was next to Thorn, and Nate stopped on the other side of Asher. Ezra trotted to my side and faced the room, sitting on his hind legs beside the throne that was mine.

I was queen.

Queen to all of the people before me.

That was if they accepted the changes I was about to make.

With a clear, tremor-free voice, I called out, "My heart beats, my eyes shine with red and black, my strength is something to be feared." I brought forward my powers, even when previously I'd been apprehensive to use them, show them, but I knew now that transforming communicated to the people the power I had. It also showed everyone, especially my mates, I would accept them in any form they came. So I changed my eyes for all to see. I grew my claws, holding them out and away for people to witness, my teeth lengthened, and around them, I voiced distinctly, "My name is Paige Alice, and I am the new ghoul queen. Your queen."

"My queen" was shouted back, and most bowed their heads in respect. Some didn't, and I understood why. Half of them wouldn't trust me, some of them wouldn't respect me until I proved myself and my worth to them. I could only hope I did. Then there were the ones who hated me even before knowing me. Without a doubt, I knew the former advisers had spread the word about how I would be changing things. Those were ones I didn't care about; except they were also the ones I would keep a better eye on.

Once people were back to standing and the silence filled the room again, I pushed down my power, turning back to my human-looking self, and then said, "Please, take a seat." They did, but I didn't. I wanted all to see me, hear me. "I am sorry for the loss of the beloved former Queen Marsala. I do hope I can live up to her standards, but also precede them with my own rules and regulations.

"I believe in change. Change for the better. From what I've seen so far, things haven't progressed from the older times. With my help, my love, my kindness, I wish things to change for a happier, healthier, and peaceful future. Before I incorporate these changes, I wish for you all to know my first decree, and that was to gain new advisers." I swung my arm out Thorn's way. "Thorn Jones, Alex Smith." Then with my other arm, I gestured to my other mates. "Asher Evans and Nate Felan." I faced the front before I could get distracted by my men. "I would also like to offer the position to Alma Burnet, Clyde Rick, and Michael Dill. Please come forth if you accept the position as my adviser." Some gasped when they'd heard Michael's name. Some muttered their disgust over the change. Many just watched.

Clyde was the first to the stage. He dropped to his knees in front of me and bowed his head. "My queen, it would be an honor."

Fear throbbed inside of me. I didn't know the protocol. Did I just ask him to rise? I had a feeling it wouldn't be enough. But then a whisper of knowledge came over me, and before my mind registered it, I had my hand out in front of me. I dug my nails into my palm and turned it over to show the blood blossoming. People started whispering. Asher and Thorn's fury washed over me. In response, I sent them tranquility, enough to relax them, for them to know this was what was meant to be done.

"Take me into you, so I know you trust me, so I know you

will advise me with your best knowledge, and so I know you will care for my people as I would myself. Take me into you to earn my trust of you. It may not be easy, but it will be rewarded. You will have my ear. You will have my help. Take me into you, Clyde Rick, and become my trusted adviser. Swear your allegiance to me."

If he took my blood, I would know, to a point at least, I could trust him.

He lifted his head, revealing his fangs had dropped. He leaned forward, and I was happy to see he wasn't hesitant in his decision. When he licked the blood from my palm, a shudder ran over him. His hands fell to the floor, his head touched my feet, and again he said, "My queen."

"Rise and take a stand at my side," I ordered.

He flashed up and over to stand beside Alex. Again, I dug my nails into my palm as Michael stepped forward. I repeated what I'd said to Clyde. Michael also shuddered from accepting my blood. He took the side next to Nate. Alma, who had the help of Asher and Thorn, got to her knees. I repeated the bind while she held my hand. After she took my blood into her, she grunted, "That packs a punch." Asher and Thorn again assisted her, and she took the spot beside Clyde while Asher and Thorn moved back to my sides.

"What about the other men at your side who are your advisers?" someone called.

"They do not need to swear to me."

"Then how can we trust they have your ear?" another shouted.

It was time everyone knew anyway.

"Some already may have sensed or learned, but I will explain. Asher is a vampire, Nate is a shifter, Thorn a ghoul, and Alex a mage. I trust them all completely with my life, with my people, because they are my bonded mates."

More gasps, whispers, and talk started up around the large room. I gave everyone time to process.

"Has the bond been completed?" It was Odin who called out.

My eyes narrowed on him, and he smirked. I bit out, "That's none of your business."

"Your life is everyone's business. We have the right to know," Barrett yelled.

I clenched my jaw. They were starting shit and I didn't like it, but I would still allow it because I wanted to see where it would lead. "Thorn and Asher," I stated with pride. "Nate and Alex will be soon, *if* they are accepting of me."

"We are," they both said clearly. My heart pounded in my chest. Alex I knew wanted to be claimed fully. Nate I hadn't been sure of until then.

"That's sacrilege. Each race should stick to their own," Patrice, who had flirted with all my men, shouted. Silence fell over the room. She stepped from her spot in the second pew and moved forward. "The former queen would never allow such a thing. Shifters are lowly beings. They don't deserve the right to have your ear."

Ezra got to his feet and growled low at her.

"No one is above anyone here," I told her sharply. "I declare that in this community, people are welcome to share their time, their love with *whomever* they wish." I scowled down on her. "Even if they are from another race."

People started chattering once more, a lot sounded happy with my reveal. Some disgusted.

Her nose scrunched up. "You're a fool. Things have been in order, have been fine until you came along."

"In order? Tell me about this order when it leaves people in need of a doctor, without help or secretly loving someone they shouldn't. No one has the right to tell people who they can love. Everyone deserves assistance, no matter their race. As the new queen, I will make sure this will happen."

Patrice scoffed. Thorn stepped forward. "Have care, Patrice, on how you speak and act in front of the queen."

"Queen? What queen? For all we know, her beating heart and her eyes could just be a trick." She looked at me. "We haven't seen your strength, and if you're allowing such things to happen, I'm worried about your smarts also."

Gasps sounded around the room.

"Enough," I clipped, anger rolling through me.

She leaned in. "It won't be enough. I'm speaking for those who don't want this change. I'm speaking on behalf of those who think you're a joke." She stepped closer. "I challenge you for the right to become queen." She smirked. "I'll even take your mates off your hands. Throw away the ones who don't matter, but Asher I will keep, and I'm sure I could break the bond."

Rage stabbed and cut me open, leaving me raw and murderous. It was one thing to go at me, but my mates...

Never.

I didn't have to bring my power forward as it was already there. I let it consume me. The changes washed over me quickly. I pointed a long, sharp claw her way. "I accept your challenge," I snarled.

Patrice hissed, her own claws and fangs popping out.

"Stupid move," I heard Nate say as I slowly approached my prey. "You'll be dead in seconds. I saw the queen rip the head off a demon possessing a body. This was even before she came into the queen's power," he said it in a bored tone.

Patrice's eyes flared with fear before she looked back to me and hissed out, "Lies."

Nate laughed. "You'll see then."

Ezra growled. He too slunk forward. "Ezra, no," I said. He stopped, glaring up at me but sat back on his rump.

Lifting my foot, I took off my right heel and then the left. Some laughed, even my mates. It meant I would be shorter, but it also meant I wouldn't be wobbling all over the place or risk spraining an ankle. Even if it would heal right away, I didn't want the distraction.

Walking down the stairs, I stopped at the bottom and offered Patrice a final chance. "Are you sure you want to do this?"

Her glance was brief, but I caught her looking to Odin. So he was the one behind it.

"Yes," she hissed. "What you want to change shouldn't be. We refuse to live like the scum you want us to be."

"Us? Who's us?"

She sneered. "You'll find out." She ran at me, her claws ready to strike across my neck. She wanted my head from my body. Only she didn't anticipate me racing toward her. I ducked and slid on my knees by her. I popped up behind her and wrapped an arm around her neck before throwing her to the side. She crashed loudly into the front pews. People managed to either jump or flash out of the way.

Patrice stood, let out a screech, and charged at me with her vampire speed. It was the same dumb move. If I hadn't had Ezra helping me learn to fight, I would have been useless to protect myself. But I wasn't. My hellhound taught me well.

I dodged her hands, threaded my hand into her hair, and threw her into the air. Some clumps of hair were left behind. I looked at them in disgust and dropped them to the floor as her body landed with a thud. She shook her head and got to her feet more slowly. I knew bones would be mending.

"Do you want to stop?" I asked, giving her yet another chance, which I probably shouldn't have.

"No," she croaked. Why? What was her point? She should know she couldn't beat me. She wouldn't have my position or my mates. Never my mates. So why continue?

Patrice screamed, stomping forward just as the doors banged open. A guard, bloody and bruised, entered.

Everyone froze.

"Felnick?" Thorn bellowed. His fear rocked into me. It had me gasping as dread filled deeply into my soul.

"They tried to take them," he said.

Thorn's gaze shot down to me. My body shook in fear. Yasmin. I looked to Patrice; she didn't wipe her smug smile from her lips quick enough.

"Did they get them?" Asher boomed. His anger revved up mine.

"No," Felnick replied before he staggered forward. Michael rushed to him and held him up.

Murmurs started.

Even though I knew they were safe and my body sagged a little in relief knowing my family was still protected—and those soldiers would be rewarded for doing so—all I could see was red. Red because I was about to bathe in some blood.

In seconds, I had a hand wrapped around Patrice's neck and her back slammed into the floor. I kneeled onto her chest and heard a rib crack. "Who ordered it?" I snarled into her face.

"I-I don't k-know," she stammered.

"Who!" I screamed down at her.

Ezra howled. My gaze swung up to see him transform in front of everyone. People screamed and scattered.

"Stop," I yelled, and my voice, even over the noise, echoed around the room. People slowed and then eventually stopped. "Nate," I called since he was the closest. He came to my side and took my position over Patrice. "Do not let her move. If she does, break something each time."

He smiled. "Yes, my queen."

I approached Ezra slowly, my hands out, my heart beating chaotically. "Ezra, calm down, honey. It's okay. They're okay."

His red-tinted eyes locked onto me. I expected another howl or growl, but he whimpered instead. I looked around. Alex's eyes were purple—he was working something. Asher had Odin on his knees on the floor in front of him. Thorn stood below the stairs, keeping an eye on everything.

"Alex?" I called thickly.

"Magic. Someone is weaving a spell into the room."

"What does it do?" I demanded.

Ezra whimpered again. In his full hellhound form, he dropped to his side. The ground shook from it.

"No," I cried, rushing to him and dropping beside his head. I ran my hands over him, fingers gliding through his fur, my body shaking hard. "Ezra, fight it, please. Please." I looked up at Alex. "Help him."

His brows dipped. "I'm trying, my queen."

A new cool breeze swept my hair and dress around.

Ezra's wet, rough tongue licked at my arm. I looked down as tears clouded my vision. I blinked them away. I couldn't lose him. He was mine. Mine, dammit. No one took from me.

Yet they were.

It shattered my chest open.

"Ezra, please don't leave me." I sniffed and buried my head into his neck. Ezra's whine had me gripping him tighter. Had more tears pooling and falling.

"There!" Alex shouted. I pulled my head up to see him pointing. I searched and found Barrett huddled in a corner, his eyes closed, his lips moving in a silent spell.

"Asher," I yelled. Asher picked Odin up, threw him at Alex and then flashed to Barrett.

Ezra whimpered again. I glanced back down. He took a breath, his eyes widened, and then…. Nothing.

Book two, *A Paige out of Hell's Book*, coming soon.

Read on for a sneak peek.

PAIGE

It had been two weeks since we buried my hellhound. Two weeks and I couldn't mend the gaping hole in my chest. It remained raw and open from the loss. From the thought of never seeing Ezra who had been there from the start. He'd been by my side, right from when I climbed out of the grave the former ghoul queen had buried me in. He'd taught me to hunt, to feed, to live, and to fight.

How was I supposed to go on without him?

He wasn't just any hellhound, he'd been mine. He was smart, cheeky, and fierce.

I wanted him back.

Back rolling his eyes or laughing at me. Back with his knowing looks every time I got aroused by my bonded mates.

Yasmin, my sister, sat on the couch beside me. She tucked a stray blonde strand behind my ear. "You don't have to do this," she told me.

But I did.

I wanted to go to the dungeons where Patrice, Odin, and Barrett were being held. Where they'd been suffering and starving. I wanted to go in there so I could question them myself.

I'd let myself have time after burying Ezra to mourn, and even though my heart remained broken, I wanted answers. They'd caused this hole inside me. They'd killed my hellhound. I wanted them to pay a hell of a lot more than they were. They'd taken someone I cared for away from me. There wasn't a chance I'd let that go unpunished.

"I do," I answered, my voice cold.

"Paige, please let your mates handle it," she pleaded.

I stood, shaking my head. "I'm the queen, Yasmin. If I want answers, I will do the work to get them. They took Ezra. They broke a piece of me. They will suffer by my hand, and it will show others what will happen if they try to take from me again."

After a moment, she stood, nodded, and took me in for a hug. "Okay," she whispered.

After I returned her embrace, I faced my mates at the door to my family's suite. I walked to them. Alex was the first to reach out and take my hand. They had been amazing since... since we lost Ezra. I hadn't as yet finalized the bond with Nate or Alex, like I already had with Asher and Thorn. But they never pushed me. They knew I wasn't in the right frame of mind. Instead, my sweet, amazing men held me when I cried, comforting me all the time. They even distracted me when I needed it. Nate did it by pissing me off. Alex when he showed me some magic. Thorn and Asher when they spoke of things happening around the castle. They'd even worked out with me daily on new fighting tactics. Nate had been the one to suggest it, saying I needed to gain some muscle on my puny body. We'd sparred right away after that comment, and I realized how good it felt. Not only did it take my mind off things, but my body also ached in a way that exhausted me. It was that night I slept for the first time.

My mates were perfect.

Especially when they were dealing with an overemotional woman.

But I wasn't sure I would ever get over losing Ezra. The loss had darkened me inside, and I held onto it, that blackness, because I refused to move on and forget him.

As Asher opened the door, he called back to Yasmin, "We'll have her back soon."

"Take care of her," she said.

"Always," Thorn replied before he stepped out the door first. Then I went, still holding Alex's hand. Asher and Nate walked out after me. Outside of the room, Thorn's men, my personal guards, surrounded us as we silently made our way down underneath the castle's floors and into the cold, damp dungeons.

Some of the guards stayed at the entrance while one opened the locked gated door and we walked in. He shut the door and stayed by it. We traveled to the end of the hall. I wanted to start with Patrice first. I had a feeling she would be weaker than Odin or Barrett. Along the way, I happened to glance into a cell and saw Malvina, the ghoul who'd disrespected me and had wanted Thorn for herself. I sent a questioning glance at Thorn who was looking at me, he said, "No one speaks to you that way, my queen."

I nodded. "Get one of the guards to see if she's learned her lesson. If he thinks she has, set her free but keep an eye on her." Afterall, I had a feeling her disrespect was rooted in her love for Thorn. I couldn't fault her for that. Although, if she didn't learn to back off and leave him alone, knowing we were bonded, then things would be hard for her.

He dipped his chin. "Yes, my queen."

As I stood by the door, I stared in through the silver bars to Patrice. No longer was she made up to perfection. Now she wore a tattered dress. Her messy hair hung limply around her dirt-caked face, and smudges of grime painted her body. But it was her glowing eyes that told me she was starving for blood. She hadn't had any in over two weeks. She was young for a vampire, which I'd learned meant she had to feed more regularly.

The door opened, and she flinched as I entered. Asher and Nate were at my back while Alex and Thorn stopped near the inside of the door, in case she got by the three of us first. I doubted it completely. There was no way I would allow it.

Stepping close to her, I looked down in disgust and unfiltered hate. "Who else was in on this?"

She laughed dryly. "No one."

"Patrice, one last chance. Who else was in on this?"

Her upper lip raised. "You're pathetic."

Bending, I gripped the knife I'd stored in my boot, lifted it, and sliced it across her neck. Her blood sprayed out, covering me. Her eyes widened, and she gagged on her own blood.

"Bag," I ordered. Someone dropped a blood bag into my waiting hand. I slapped it to her mouth, and she drank greedily. Her neck knitted back together. "Who else, Patrice?"

"Fuck you," she rasped.

In response, I threw the bagged blood on the dust-covered ground. She cried out, until I sliced her newly healed neck open again. That time, I waited. I let her suffer by carving her neck open over and over while it tried to heal.

"Bag," I clipped. Another was deposited in my hand. "Who else, Patrice?"

"Selma," she whispered.

Before she drank all the blood down, I took it from her and dropped it to the floor.

"No!" she cried.

I shook my head. "You shouldn't have been a part of it.

You should have stayed well away from me. Instead, you took from me. You helped kill Ezra. For that, you will suffer." I turned and walked away, catching a guard's eyes. "Keep doing what I was. Until I say otherwise."

He bowed. Respect shone in his eyes. "Yes, my queen."

"And send someone after Selma. I want her down here."

"As you wish, my queen," another guard answered, and three of them peeled away from the wall outside Patrice's cell to do as I bid.

I would make a mockery of them, and make sure no one wanted to deal with my wrath again while I was at it.

As I moved toward Barrett's cell, worry seeped into my mind. Already I'd hardened myself to a point where a part of my innocence withered away. There were vile creatures out there, even within these walls, and it was up to me to deal with them. I had to be strong; I had to steal a fortress around my own emotions sometimes. What worried me the most about it, about this newer unbreakable side to me, was if my mates would despise seeing me like that and the queen I was becoming? Would they hate me? Would they find what I did disgusting? I could have had them handle this for me. They would have. They were used to fighting, killing, but I didn't want them to touch her. To have spoken with her. Did they understand why I had to deal with these vermin myself? I wanted to make them hurt, like I had the people I'd killed to feed, the ones with evil intent, and the ones Ezra had taught me to hunt.

Ezra. My chest speared with sorrow. I bit my bottom lip to stop the emotion taking hold.

Did my mates, the men who were made for me and me for them, understand I bloodied myself for Ezra? He had to be avenged, and I had to be the one to do it.

Would they think of me different because of these events?

"Never, love," Asher answered quietly. "You are beautiful and amazing. No matter what side you show us, we will always want you." Lately, he and Thorn kept their emotions locked away from me since I'd already been feeling so much, but they opened themselves wide. Hope, love, pride, even arousal crawled over and inside of me from them.

"Thank you." I let my gratitude show in my voice. I doubted there would be a day I wouldn't feel lucky to have my mates. Yes, even Nate.

Another guard opened the cell door. Stepping through, I looked down at Barrett on his cot in the corner of the room. He was in the same shape as Patrice, but being a mage, he hungered for food and water instead. He sat up quickly and curled into himself.

"Leave me alone!" he cried. I glanced at his ankle. It still held the device that took away his magic.

I shook my head. "I can't. I won't. Ezra was mine, and you killed him. Where do you think that leaves you?"

"Y-You can't kill me. I was protecting the people from that beast."

Lies. I could scent it. "No one knew what he was. As far as people knew, he was a dog. And *mine*," I said, low and harsh. "Why did you kill him?"

He shook his head.

When I stepped closer, he shouted, "What did you do to Patrice?"

"You'll find out if you don't talk, because I'll do the same to you." I gestured down my body. "You see her blood. Do you want yours to join hers?"

He quivered. His scent shifted. Sweat and fear. He opened his mouth and said quietly, "Since your family was safe, I tried to take matters into my own hands. The spell wouldn't work on your mates—"

"You tried?" I bellowed. My powers surged, my eyes glowed, my claws and teeth extended.

He whimpered and tried to scuttle back, but he was already in the corner. I enjoyed seeing and scenting his terror. He deserved it.

"They were safe. You were safe. I couldn't touch anyone but the mutt."

"Shit," I heard Alex curse behind me.

Facing Alex, I saw dread dipping his brows, darkening his eyes, slumping his shoulders. "What?" I asked.

He bowed his head, eyes to the floor. "It's my fault, my queen."

"Look at me," I ordered softly. He straightened. "What are you saying, Alex?"

I could tell he wanted to move his gaze away from me. Guilt flickered in his eyes, but his focus stayed on me when he said, "I layered a spell over us and you. I should have for Ezra, but I didn't think." His jaw clenched. "It's my fault he got to him."

"No," I stated, resolute. I pulled my power in and took the steps to be in front of Alex. I cupped his cheeks, staring into his agonized gaze. "It's not your fault. Never your fault. It's theirs. They wanted to hurt me, hurt all of my mates, but couldn't because *you* protected us."

"But I should have—"

"Don't take on that blame. *Please.* It's not your fault." Truth carried my words. I wouldn't blame Alex and didn't want him to blame himself either. I could only hope he heard the certainty in my voice. I would have shared it in my emotions with him, but we'd yet to finalize the bond. Something that would change and soon; I needed my mates. It would be safer for all of us to be connected completely. I wanted all them to know that even through my grief they're mine, something I hadn't shown them since we'd lost Ezra. They needed to know I would protect them, I would love them, and I would kill for them.

It was Barrett, Odin, Patrice, and Selma's fault. They were all guilty for the event.

"Okay," he said in an exhale.

Smiling, I nodded. "Okay." Leaning up, I brushed my lips against his. His heart galloped from the first touch of my lips.

"Hellhounds should be able to repel magic thrown at them. Why didn't that happen?" Thorn interrupted; I was sure it was more to himself than everyone. However, it had me turning back to Barrett.

He shook his head. "I don't know how it worked. I don't."

Maybe Ezra was different from any other hellhound. It was all I could think of.

Brushing the thought away, for now, I moved back toward Barrett and called over my shoulder, "Asher."

"Yes, my queen?"

"I need you to help me with something because I have a feeling he won't tell the truth, no matter what I do."

Asher stepped to my side as we stopped in front of Barrett. "Make him tell me if he's romantically involved with Odin."

Barrett let out a noise and buried his head into his knees, crying over and over, "No."

I was glad when Asher's eyes bled to green, and his fangs dropped. Thankfully, my libido didn't kick into hyperdrive—it certainly wasn't the time. The room chilled as his power thickened throughout.

Asher leaned forward a little. His voice was soft, almost lulling when he said, "Look at me."

Barrett shook his head repeatedly.

"Look at me," Asher's voice deepened.

Slowly, Barrett lifted his head and gazed into Asher's eyes. "Is Odin your lover?"

"Yes."

Asher sucked his power back in, and he returned to his human appearance as he moved back. Barrett blinked over and over, coming out of the trance Asher had put him in.

"I thought so," I said.

"What? You talk about changing things, and you're against me loving a man?"

I laughed humorlessly. "No. You have it wrong. I'm all about people loving whoever they want. But... you took someone *I* loved."

His eyes widened as understanding registered. He paled, and his heart beat erratically. "No." He gasped. "This is different. He was just a damn hellhound."

"Ezra was family!" I yelled, my hands balling into fists. Over my shoulder, I ordered, "Bring Odin in here."

"Please, no. Please don't do this. I love him."

"I love Ezra. If I'd begged, would you have dropped the spell? Would you have let me save him?"

His lips snapped closed.

Yeah, I didn't think so.

"Stop, unhand me," we heard shouted. "You can't do this to me. I have rights. I am an adviser."

I turned enough to see Odin being forced through the doorway by two guards. He looked in the same state as his lover. His ankles and hands were chained together. Only he still held a note of stubbornness, or arrogance and distaste.

His face screwed up at the sight of me. "What's the meaning of this?"

With speed behind me, I swiftly moved behind Odin, gripped his head, and using my queen strength, I ripped it from his shoulders. More blood sprayed out, coating me. Barrett started screaming when Odin's body fell to the floor. I threw Odin's head over near Barrett.

"A life for a life," I called loudly. Barrett keened and rocked on his bed. I didn't sense any repulsion from Asher or Thorn. I even glanced to Alex and Nate, but to my shock, they showed understanding. Nate nodded.

"My queen," someone said.

Turning, I saw Felnick standing in the doorway. "Yes?" I asked.

"You have a call. It's important."

"Now?"

"Yes, my queen."

"Who is it?" Thorn asked.

"Lucifer."

What the fuckety-fuck?

ACKNOWLEDGMENTS

Thank you to the readers who have stuck with me as I travel down a different path.

Also, thanks to *all new readers* for taking a chance on me and trying my work for the first time.

To *Becky*, my amazing, pushy editor from *Hot Tree Editing*, thank you for always bringing out the best in me. I couldn't do any of this without you!

Andreea, thank you so darn much for such an amazing digital illustration for the cover.

Lee Ching, thank you for your work on the cover, the teasers and for your formatting skills.

I'll always appreciate the indie world and how amazing authors can be. A big shout out to *Jaymin Eve, Montana Ash, Raven Kennedy, Ivy Asher, Tate James, TL Smith, and Maria-Lisa deMora.*

I can never go by without thanking my sister, *Rachel Morgan*, especially for being my sounding board.

When I first started writing *A Torn Paige*, I was so scared it was all wrong and I didn't know if I should continue. I made her read the very rough first few chapters and with her encouragement—where she called me crazy and told me to get my ass into finishing the rest because she needed it—so I just had to complete the project.

MORE BOOKS
Titles under L. Rose

<u>Hidden Kingdom Trilogy</u>
A Torn Paige
A Lost Paige
A Final Paige (releasing February 2020)

MORE BOOKS
Titles under Lila Rose

Romance
<u>Hawks MC: Ballarat Charter</u>
Holding Out (FREE)
Climbing Out
Finding Out (novella)
Black Out
No Way Out
Coming Out (m/m novella)
(They're also available in box sets in KU)

<u>Hawks MC: Caroline Springs Charter</u>

The Secret's Out
Hiding Out
Down and Out
Living Without
Walkout (novella)
Hear Me Out (m/m)
Breakout (novella)
Fallout
(They're also available in box sets in KU)

Romantic Comedies
Making Changes
Making Sense

Fumbled Love

Paranormal
In The Dark (standalone)

ABOUT THE AUTHOR

Find L.Rose online
www.lilarosebooks.com/
Facebook:
bit.ly/2du0taO
Instagram:
instagram.com/lilarose78
email: lilarose2678@gmail.com

www.ingramcontent.com/pod-product-compliance
Lightning Source LLC
Chambersburg PA
CBHW070017120726
47909CB00003B/972